W9-BLL-409

THE TURNING

WITHDRAWN
REDWOOD
LIBRARY

The Turning

Gillian Chan

KCP Fiction

KCP Fiction is an imprint of Kids Can Press

Text © 2005 Gillian Chan

All rights reserved. No part of this publication may be reproduced, stored in a retrieval system or transmitted, in any form or by any means, without the prior written permission of Kids Can Press Ltd. or, in case of photocopying or other reprographic copying, a license from The Canadian Copyright Licensing Agency (Access Copyright). For an Access Copyright license, visit www.accesscopyright.ca or call toll free to 1-800-893-5777.

This is a work of fiction and any resemblance of characters to persons living or dead is purely coincidental.

Many of the designations used by manufacturers and sellers to distinguish their products are claimed as trademarks. Where those designations appear in this book and Kids Can Press Ltd. was aware of a trademark claim, the designations have been printed in initial capital letters (e.g., Ouija).

Kids Can Press acknowledges the financial support of the Government of Ontario, through the Ontario Media Development Corporation's Ontario Book Initiative; the Ontario Arts Council; the Canada Council for the Arts; and the Government of Canada, through the BPIDP, for our publishing activity.

The author wishes to acknowledge the financial support of the Ontario Arts Council and the Canada Council for the Arts in the writing of this novel.

ONTARIO ARTS COUNCIL
CONSEIL DES ARTS DE L'ONTARIO

Canada Council for the Arts Conseil des Arts du Canada

Published in Canada by
Kids Can Press Ltd.
29 Birch Avenue
Toronto, ON M4V 1E2

Published in the U.S. by
Kids Can Press Ltd.
2250 Military Road
Tonawanda, NY 14150

www.kidscanpress.com

Edited by Charis Wahl
Designed by Marie Bartholomew
Frontispiece carving/photo of "Mirth" © Walter S. Arnold

Printed and bound in Canada

CM 05 0 9 8 7 6 5 4 3 2 1
CM PA 05 0 9 8 7 6 5 4 3 2 1

National Library of Canada Cataloguing in Publication Data

Chan, Gillian
The turning / written by Gillian Chan.

ISBN 1-55337-575-0 (bound). ISBN 1-55337-576-9 (pbk.)

I. Title.

PS8555.H39243T87 2004 jC813'.54 C2004-903114-7

Kids Can Press is a Corus™ Entertainment company

MAR 12 2009

Young Adult
FICTION

177234

Y CHA Chan, Gillian

~~31332002792067~~

For fathers and their sons, especially those dear to my heart

September

Tuesday

"Fi-ight! Fi-ight! Fi-ight!"

It had started out as a sinister whisper, but now the chanting was swelling to a roar as the crowd strained for the best view.

A blur of faces surrounded Ben Larsson, focused on him with an eager anticipation that was frighteningly primitive.

He shrugged. The casual gesture masked the throbbing fear inside. Ben struggled to make himself heard. "Look, this is all a mistake." He grimaced, hating the weak threadiness of his voice. "I don't want to fight. Hell, I don't even know this guy. If I've offended him, I'm sorry." Ben tried to push his way through the crowd, but it was like walking into a brick wall, so solid was the crush. Hands roughly pushed him back into the circle. His opponent, a stocky boy, bounced on his toes, his fists loosely clenched. He grinned at Ben.

Why was this happening?

Ben's thoughts whirled, desperately seeking an explanation. It was only Ben's second day at this lousy school — which he'd been determined to hate, of course. This whole damn England trip was his dad's idea, so Ben was doing his best to make it a nightmare. The only sick pleasure he got these days was seeing Lars tie himself in knots trying to please him. Ben didn't have a death wish, though — he'd been keeping his head down, not letting the kids know what he really thought of them and their pathetic school.

The boy assigned to show him around yesterday had stuck with him just long enough to make sure that Ben knew where he had to be and when. This morning, he had given Ben a halfhearted wave in the lower sixth common room, but had then left him glowering in the corner. That had suited Ben just fine, until now — he could do with a friendly face now.

A flicker of movement drew his attention. His opponent was shadow boxing — quick, powerful jabs that Ben could almost hear as the fists pushed through the air. Ben swallowed and tried again. "What *is* all this? What am I supposed to have done?"

A voice rose above the crowd. "The Yank's chicken!" Clucking noises gradually drowned out the chant of "Fi-ight!"

Damn right I'm chicken, thought Ben, recalling the only punch he had ever thrown. When his grandfather had told him, after his mother's death, that he would be going to Winnipeg to live with his dad, he had lashed out, putting his fist through the plasterboard of his bedroom wall. The bruised and bleeding knuckles had provided cover for the sobs that lay in wait for him, always there now under the angry mask he presented to the world.

Tentatively, he curled his fingers into fists. An excited exhalation came from the crowd as if Ben's gesture was the signal that something was finally about to happen. The other boy danced forward, still shadow boxing, his wide grin at odds with the hard calculation and strangely knowing look in his eyes. Ben backed away, trying to buy time, frantically searching through the events that had brought him to this.

It had all been so innocuous. Shouldering his backpack, Ben had set off for the bus stop, his head down, thinking about how boring the day had been. The school computers were crap and the teacher knew less about programming than Ben did. He hadn't been looking where he was going, so the collision might have been his fault, but it had been little more than a brush in passing. Ben had looked up, mumbled an apology, and a hand shot out and grabbed the front of his sweatshirt.

"What did you say?"

Ben had found himself looking down at a boy considerably shorter than himself, probably younger, too, as he was in uniform, which the sixth formers didn't have to wear. Putting up his hands to indicate his good intent, Ben had repeated his apology, suddenly aware that there was a semicircle of boys around them, perhaps friends of the boy who held on to him. One of them sneered, "Do you understand what he's saying, Baz? He talks funny. I think he's taking the piss!"

Baz had squinted up at Ben. "I think you're right, Kenny. I don't think he's sorry at all, are you, mate?"

Ben had stuttered that he was, but the boys had started the chant, the one that worked like a magic call, bringing people running.

A painful jab in the kidney made Ben wince. He could back up no farther. He looked around to see who had punched him. Kenny grinned malevolently back. "Chicken!" he mouthed.

Baz took advantage of his distraction to punch him hard in the stomach, following it up with a fist to the side of the jaw. As Ben tried to swallow the rush of saliva, he felt his legs give way. With a grin, Baz brought up his right knee, connecting solidly with Ben's chin, snapping his head back. Blood joined the spit and he fell to the ground, winded.

Ben retched weakly. His eyes were clenched shut with the pain, so he sensed rather than saw the crowd leaving. Forcing them open, Ben saw watery blue sky, then, too close to his own was a girl's face, pale as milk, framed by an unruly mass of fiery red hair. The girl was talking to him, her face contorted and urgent — but no sound could penetrate the throbbing hiss filling his head, which increased when the girl grasped his shoulders and shook him. Waves of pain enveloped Ben, and he sank away into a place where he need no longer think.

"Ben? Ben Larsson! My god, what happened to you?" Peering down at him was the ruddy face of his year tutor, Mr. Greengrass, who knelt in the mud seemingly careless of his khaki pants. "Can you sit up?"

Ben was surprised to find that he could, even though he still found it difficult to catch his breath and waves of nausea left him feeling cold and clammy. He shook his head, trying to clear it, but the movement sent sharp, flaring pain up his jaw. He groaned, a ragged sound that caused Mr. Greengrass to wince and place his arm around Ben's shoulders. "Let's get you inside. Then we can assess the damage and you can tell me what happened." As he gingerly hauled Ben to his feet, Greengrass kept up a torrent of talk. "I was just going to my car when I saw the crowd. Any teacher knows a crowd like that is not good. As soon as I headed over, yelling, they took off. If only I had come out earlier."

No kidding, Ben thought, as he tried to get his story into some form that would make Greengrass leave him alone. It crossed his mind that he could drop the toad who'd attacked him in deep shit. He'd heard his name, and that of his buddy, Kenny, but experience warned him that this might bring more trouble than it was worth. He'd stick to the code of schools everywhere: never rat.

Despite his throbbing jaw, Ben no longer felt as if he was going to throw up. “I’m okay now, Mr. Greengrass. I’ll just go catch my bus, clean up at home,” he said, surprised when the words came out thickly, nothing like his normal voice at all.

“No, Ben. Just listen to yourself. You’ve got a knot on the side of your jaw the size of an egg. We need to check you out.” Mr. Greengrass ignored his protests, subtly increasing the pressure of the arm around Ben’s shoulders and guiding him toward the school.

Ben found himself bundled into and left in a bleak little first aid room, furnished with a cot, a cupboard of medical supplies and a teacher he had never seen before but who seemed to know what he was doing. He cleaned up Ben’s face, got him to swill out his mouth, drawing his breath in sharply at the mixture of ropey saliva and blood. With gentle fingers, he probed Ben’s jaw. Ben winced, but the pain was less than it had been.

“Nothing broken, but it’s definitely going to hurt awhile. Open your mouth so I can see what the damage is.” Feeling foolish, Ben complied. “Ah, splendid. No teeth broken, and you bit your tongue, but didn’t cut through it.” Seeing Ben’s eyes widen, the teacher gave a grim laugh. “Oh, it happens, believe me, especially when you get kneed like that.” He looked as if he was going to say more, but a gentle tap on the door and the appearance of Mr. Greengrass's head around it stopped him.

"How is he, Barry? Should we take him to the hospital to be checked over?"

"Nothing's broken. I think he had the air knocked out of him more than anything. A cut tongue and some bruises, but he'll live."

Annoyance flashed through Ben. They talked about him like he was a little kid who couldn't be trusted to speak up for himself. When Barry suddenly thrust three fingers in front of Ben's face and demanded to know how many he was holding up, Ben had to fight down the urge to say "Eight!"

"Three," he muttered sullenly.

A pat on the back was his reward, but the teacher added, "No sign of concussion, but tell his dad to keep an eye on him tonight." Shit! They'd called Lars. That was all Ben needed.

His worst fears were confirmed when Mr. Greengrass helped him to his feet, saying, "Your father's on his way, Ben, but he will be a while yet, so come to my office and we'll have a chat about what happened."

Ben had been in Mr. Greengrass's office once before, when Lars had brought him in to sign up for his courses just before term had started, but then he had been concentrating on being difficult. He had kept his eyes on the faded brown carpet and kept his contributions to "I guess so" or, for more of an edge, "If you say so." He had expected Lars to explode on the way home, but all Lars had done was shake his shaggy head and say, "You're your own worst enemy, Ben. It's not a life sentence — you're just here for my sabbatical, so why not enjoy the year? It's a clean start, a new country — maybe just what we both need."

Ben hadn't bothered to reply. What was the point? No one bothered to ask what he wanted — that was why he was here with Lars. The old, familiar anger welled up inside him and he forced it down, trying to distract himself by looking around Greengrass's room. It was nicer than he had expected. One entire wall was lined with books, and not just boring texts on educational psychology. There were books on history, too, which Greengrass taught, including a lot of local history and folklore. Ben suppressed a snort. No wonder Lars had liked him so much. On the wall between two windows was a really weird poster, full of twisting tree roots and what appeared to be wizened and deformed people. Ben shuddered. The tangled, curving roots pulled your eye to a small, central figure — a powerful man holding an ax, ready to strike.

Mr. Greengrass coughed, trying to get Ben's attention. "Ben, I need you to tell me what happened. As everyone was running off, I'm sure I recognized some of the usual suspects." He flushed slightly. "Don't get the wrong idea, though. This sort of thing doesn't happen often." He stared hard as if willing Ben to speak.

"It all happened so quickly," Ben said, suppressing a smile. Look! I'm a walking cliché. He couldn't resist adding, "I was walking along, minding my own business, when someone bumped into me, or I bumped into him. I'm not sure. I apologized and he grabbed me. One of his friends said I talked funny and was making fun of him." The look on Mr. Greengrass's face showed that he knew he was being handed a pile of crap, so fresh it was steaming, but what could he do? Ben knew he had to give Greengrass the bare bones, but nothing that would enable him to identify the attacker. "This kid's friends started yelling, and then there was a crowd. I tried to reason with him, tried to get away, but they wouldn't let me out of the circle. I got distracted and then he hit me." For effect, Ben felt his jaw, the wince when his fingers touched the point of impact only slightly exaggerated. "I don't remember much after that — till I saw you." There was a girl, he thought. A girl. He knew that he shouldn't mention the girl. Her red hair was so striking, drifting snakelike around her small face, that Greengrass would have no trouble finding her, questioning her. Who the hell was she? Some weirdo who got her kicks out of ministering to fight victims?

No. Her panicked urgency, her obvious fear pulled at Ben in a way that he couldn't explain.

Mr. Greengrass sighed, clearly irritated by Ben's extended silence.

"Was it anyone from your classes? You're taking English, Computer Science, Music and Maths, aren't you, Ben?"

Ben said, "I'd never seen the kid before. He was younger, I think, because he was in uniform. Shorter than me, brown hair." Ben thought this was vague enough, but Greengrass's expression was too much like a look of recognition.

"Did you hear a name when his friends were talking, Ben?"

Ben was saved from lying by the office door swinging open as Lars burst in, filling the room with a rush of sound and energy.

"Ben, are you all right? What the hell happened?" Lars' baritone bounced around the office as he hunkered down and ran his hands over Ben's face. Ben pulled away and leaned back into his chair, trying to put as much distance between himself and his father as he could. As if Lars really cared, Ben thought.

"He's a bit battered and shaken, I think, Dr. Larsson, but nothing serious."

Greengrass immediately went up in Ben's estimation as his distaste for Lars' histrionics showed clearly on his face. When Lars started his rambling lecture on the Icelandic patronymic system of names — how Ben was Ben Larsson, because he was Lars' son, while he, Lars, took his father's name and was Tryggvason — he interrupted brusquely, "Yes, quite. You did explain all that before. I forgot. I'm sorry. What's more important is that I'm trying to establish what happened; but, unfortunately, Ben seems to have been the victim of an unprovoked attack by someone he didn't know." Mr. Greengrass looked relieved when Lars finally sat on the chair next to Ben. "I can assure you that we will do everything we can to find the culprits and punish them accordingly."

"I should hope so." Lars' voice shook.

Ben looked sideways at Lars, thinking that he was overacting the role of worried father. Where the hell had he been when Ben broke his leg in grade three? Not even a phone call. There was sweat on Lars' face and his usual ruddy complexion was pale. Give the man an Oscar, Ben thought sardonically, then stared at the carpet in the hope that both Lars and Greengrass would leave him alone.

"I chose this school because my colleagues at the university recommended it highly." Lars leaned forward, his voice taking on a confiding, almost conspiratorial tone. "As you know from our discussion, life has thrown some hard knocks at Ben recently ..."

Ben no longer heard what Lars was saying. A tide of rage boiled up inside him. Just what the hell did Greengrass "know," and when did Lars tell him? As far as Ben knew, the only time Lars had met Greengrass was the day Ben signed up for his classes. He stood up abruptly. "I want to go now. I want to go home." Ben turned and walked out of the office, shaking. He leaned against the cold, cream wall of the corridor, fighting to control his breathing.

It was some minutes before Lars appeared. He tried to put his arm around Ben's shoulders, but Ben shook it off and strode down the hall.

Lars' car was parked on the double yellow lines just outside the entrance, its butt end sticking out. Despite his anger, Ben couldn't help smiling. It really was the most ridiculous car — bright green, tiny and snub-nosed, like a child's drawing. Lars had bought it, sight unseen, from a professor who was heading off to America. He had been seduced by its name, Ka. "It's a Ford," he had said, with a breezy wave of the hand. He had grinned at Ben. "You know what a ka is, don't you?" When Ben hadn't answered, he had said, "It's an Egyptian term for the soul. Isn't that a blast, driving around in a soul car made by a corporate bloodsucker?" When he finally saw the car, Lars looked like a kid who had had his candy taken from him. Watching him squeezing his huge, bulky body into it gave Ben pleasure every time, especially as Lars did it grimly and without complaint. It made up for Ben having to fold himself up like a lawn chair to get his long legs into it.

"Come on, Benny. It's open." Lars had caught up and hovered solicitously at his side.

"Don't call me Benny!" Ben growled. In those first few weeks with Lars in Winnipeg, he had said that so often he thought he would go mad. Only his mom called him Benny, and no one else would, not ever.

"Sorry, sorry." Lars levered himself into the car. "Stress. It's not every day you get pulled out of a meeting because your kid has been beaten up — and on his second day at school in a new country." He looked sideways at Ben as he fitted the key into the ignition. "So what happened? Really happened, I mean? I assume you were your usual close-mouthed self with Mr. Greengrass."

"Just what he told you, Lars." Ben stared out of the window, watching the small houses flash by as Lars deftly guided the car out onto the ring road that would take them home to Cringleford. "A kid I'd never seen before picked a fight. I didn't cause it. I didn't fight back. It was all over very fast."

"But why would he do that?" Lars ran a meaty hand through his thick hair.

"Who knows? He was smaller than me, but tough — maybe he thought it was a challenge, going after the big new kid. Maybe he doesn't like Canadians." Ben laughed. "Only, he and his buddies thought I was a Yank. Maybe it's some rite of passage thing, maybe every new kid gets beaten up their first week. Maybe it's a hallowed tradition Greengrass likes to keep quiet." Greengrass's name brought Ben's anger back. "Which reminds me, Lars, just when the hell did you two have this nice chat about 'the hard knocks' life has thrown at me?" Ben stared at Lars.

Lars didn't take his eyes off the road, but a faint flush colored his cheeks. "I called him, okay? So sue me. I was worried about how you'd get on, so I called and told him about ... your mom, and how you had been finding it hard to come to terms with your, uh, new circumstances."

"Circumstances!" Ben exploded. "How fucking mealymouthed can you get?" He kicked angrily at the car mat. "Mom died, Lars. That's not a fucking circumstance. She died. She was in pain for three months before she went off her head with the goddamn drugs they were pumping into her. And, Lars, part of that pain was knowing that when she died, you'd come back into my life. I'd seen you like once since you decided that you weren't cut out to be married and a father. And then only when you were changing planes in Toronto and Mom drove me out to the airport. You hugged me and I cried, or so Mom told me. Did you write? Did you call? Hell, no! Just fourteen birthday cards." Ben sneered, his face twisting with pain as he thought of those cards, dog-eared and held together with a rubber band, hidden in his sock drawer. "'Happy Birthday, Ben. Love Lars.' Always the same. Oh, yes, and a check. Paid up for another year." Ben knew that he was shouting and struggled for control. "So, imagine my surprise when Grandpa told me that I'd be living with you — didn't ask, didn't consult, just told me. What changed your mind, Lars? Did you think a sixteen-year-old would be easier than a two-year-old?" A bitter laugh escaped Ben. "That was naive, wasn't it? Now you wish you hadn't insisted I come to you instead of staying with Mom's parents, right? I bet you still think that it's going to work out in the end. Sorry, Lars, there are no happy fucking endings. You think I'm difficult? Well, you ain't seen nothing yet!" Ben glared across at Lars, wanting him to yell back. He'd got him angry, all right. A vein was throbbing in Lars' forehead, and his knuckles were white on the steering wheel as he swung the car to a screeching halt, spraying gravel, on the open space in front of the cottage.

Lars slowly put his hands in his lap before he turned as far as he was able in the close confines of the car. His blue eyes were blazing with a hard, wet sheen.

Ben flinched, waiting for the great bellow that he knew Lars could produce.

"I *didn't* ask for you, Ben." The words, delivered in almost a hiss, dropped like pebbles into the silence. "Janine wanted her parents to be your guardians, but they felt they couldn't cope at their age, given the way you'd been ... acting out. That gave her no option but me, even though she hated the whole goddamn idea. I'm Lars the bogeyman, remember? I am the bastard who ruined her life, which I know she told anyone who'd listen, including you, Ben. Including you. And that's the thing I find hard to forgive." Lars' voice died away, and he seemed lost.

Ben stared, hollow, a great void inside him that would never be filled. His tongue was frozen.

Covering his eyes with his hands, Lars shook his head like a bear being worried by dogs. "Ah, shit, I shouldn't have, not like this, Ben. I wanted you. I swear I've always wanted to be part of your life, but your mother was never going to let that happen. When your grandfather called to say that Janine was ill, I assumed they'd become your guardians. When she called and asked me to take you, I didn't believe her at first. I thought it was some cruel joke, until she explained. I could hardly speak. This was my chance — to put things right. This whole trip to England seemed so right, too. Time for us to get to know each other away from ... our normal lives. I was so happy, Ben, so bloody happy." Lars peered at Ben's white face. "Aaagh! I've handled this badly. But you got me so mad. I'm sorry, Ben. I'm so sorry." He reached out to pat Ben's arm, but Ben was already half out of the car.

The gravel shifted and Ben almost lost his balance. Fighting for a foothold, he turned and ran, as fast and hard as he could, from the neat row of gentrified cottages, over the field and into the thick wood.

The boy was back.

The one whose heart flame sang out to Wyliff. It was full of rage, but shot through with a power that Wyliff recognized, a power that bore the mark of the one man who understood, back when men still saw. This boy had his blood, the blood of the smith.

Wyliff watched him lope around the clearing, hacking at the tall grass with a branch he'd ripped from a sapling.

"Goddamn it to hell!" The shout so scared Wyliff that it took all his will not to bolt from the cover of the trees. The leaves in his hair quivered with distress. He felt the vines around his arms and legs tighten. Had the boy sensed something? He was heading straight for Wyliff's hiding place. Not daring to move, Wyliff closed his eyes, knowing that their russet-green flash could give him away.

The boy was very close. Wyliff could smell him, unnatural and sharp against the warm aroma of earth and decaying leaves. The boy moved past. Wyliff started to breathe again, a soft susurration like a breeze, catching in his throat when the boy's outer covering snagged on a cracked piece of Wyliff's skin. The material felt alien, soft, like fur, but it had never breathed, never lived. Wyliff couldn't control the shudder that ran through his elongated limbs, but he stifled the urge to claw himself free.

Angrily, the boy jerked away.

Wyliff delicately sniffed — salt water, on the boy's face. The smell lingered even after the boy crashed off blindly through the trees.

Movement came back gradually. Wyliff twitched and shook until he felt the sap rise. Then he sighed. Trees, leaves, small animals scurrying in the undergrowth — all was once again right with his world, but now there was promise here. The boy could be useful.

A breeze stirred his hair, rattled his leaves. Something nagged at him. Wyliff's thin, knobby fingers flinched from the small tuft that stuck to the hard skin of his leg. He brought it up in front of his face, his eyes narrowing at the way it glowed — the lurid green he associated with dead things. Carefully, he placed it on the palm of his other hand. Pursing his lips, he blew, sending the stuff spinning into the air like dandelion fluff. Wyliff's face cracked into a huge smile, stirring the foliage of his beard, as he chased after it.

Every window seemed to be lit up and none of the curtains were drawn. The cottage was like a movie set. The light reflected off the polished surfaces of the wooden furniture with just the right touch of rusticity. Professor Parker, who had rented the place to them, had glowed with quiet pride as he told them how he and his wife had haunted auctions and antique shops. Seeing the size of Lars and Ben, a faint flicker of worry had crossed his face, as if he imagined the more delicate pieces breaking should they sit on them. Looking at Ben's determinedly black clothes, he had said, "You do remember the damage clause in your lease, Dr. Tryggvason?"

Ben hadn't been able to stifle a smile when Lars had replied straight-faced, "Yeah, wild parties only every other Saturday!"

Professor Parker had reared back, nostrils flaring.

"A joke, my man, just a joke," Lars had said. "Ben's the quiet type, in love with his computer, and I'm here to research and write my book. Just a couple of stay-at-home bachelors." His pat on the back had sent Parker stumbling forward.

When he had shrugged his tweed jacket back in place, Parker had managed a weak smile. "And you're happy with Mrs. Lea coming in once a week to clean?"

"Absolutely. I leave her a check for forty pounds in the morning, and when I come home the place will be spotless — that's the deal, right?" Lars had tried to look sincere and responsible, but the effect was spoiled by the tangled ponytail and the denim shirt that looked like Lars had used it to mop up spaghetti sauce. Professor Parker regarded Lars as if he were a lunatic, but he had left them to it and the cottage hadn't proved too hard to live in, even if it was in the middle of nowhere.

Ben strained for some sign of Lars. The car was outside, just as he had left it.

In the woods, Ben had heard Lars crashing around, yelling his name, but it had been easy to stay hidden. Let the bastard suffer. But the clearing Ben had found on his first exploration had felt different today. It had spooked him somehow.

The only sound was the wind rattling around the cottage. From inside, silence — none of the usual music blaring. Keeping out of sight, Ben edged through the archway into the back garden. He positioned himself under the willow tree on the lawn, caged by its hanging limbs. Autumn was taking its toll on the greenery, but Ben liked the feeling of enclosure, able to see out, but difficult to spot. From here, he could look into the kitchen. Lars was sitting at the long oak table, his head in his hands. A book was open before him, but he didn't appear to be reading it. Ben studied his father almost clinically, like you would a scientific specimen. People said that he looked more like Lars than his mother, but other than their height and light brown hair, Ben didn't see it. Lars' height was matched by bulk, solid ropelike muscle, that made him seem like some ancient warrior god — an effect that Ben suspected he cultivated with the wild, long hair and beard. His features, too, were large, seemingly carved out of rock. Ben grinned. Maybe that's why in the romance novels his mother loved to read, they often referred to the hero's face as craggy. Ben thought of his own skinny frame and soft face. Nah, nothing of Lars at all!

Suddenly, the branches of the willow shook, making a hard, staccato rattle. They twisted and intertwined. There was a noise from the far end of the garden that sounded like laughter from a voice rusty with disuse. Ben looked over his shoulder — nothing but darkness. The laughter came closer. With a yelp, Ben pushed at the willow branches, which seemed to fight back, sticking sharply into his clothing, snagging and pulling, scratching at his face and hands. Finally free, he ran for the cottage, not daring to look behind him, and almost stumbled when the door flew open and Lars stood there, his huge figure silhouetted against the light.

"Ben, you're all right!" Lars tried to hug him, but Ben twisted past his father into the safety of the kitchen.

"Look at you — your face is even more of a mess. What the hell have you been doing? You're all scratched up. What were you thinking of, running off like that? I came after you." Lars smiled ruefully and followed Ben into the kitchen. He went over to the sink and filled the kettle. His voice muffled, he said, "Look, I'm sorry for telling you about your grandparents like that. Can't we sit down and talk? We really need to." There was a pleading note in his voice. "I'll make some tea, and there's a pie in the oven ..."

"I don't want to talk, and you can shove your pie!" Ben slammed out of the kitchen and in the quiet of the hallway heard Lars say, "Great, Lars! You handled that really well!" Ben tore up the stairs, his feet thudding on the wooden steps.

Ben made his way to his bedroom window. The garden was bathed in moonlight. The willow's bare branches hung straight down as usual. He thought he saw a flicker of movement by the hedge, but the more he stared, the more he became convinced it was just the wind moving the twigs. Shrugging, he flicked on his computer and then the light.

While the computer hummed into life, Ben studied his face in the ornate mirror that hung over the corner dresser. His normally pale face had an angry-looking red lump on the side of the jawbone. The skin was taut and shiny, although the edges were already starting to turn a sickly yellow as the bruise worked its way to the surface. His hair was tangled and his face was scratched, just as Lars had said — but the scratches weren't random. Four angled lines stood out in the middle of his forehead, small beads of blood attesting to their freshness, as if someone had carved the letter W. He stared at it for a long time, only tearing himself away when the hairs on the back of his neck prickled as if someone was watching him. He pulled the curtains shut without daring to look outside. Banging the keyboard harder than necessary, Ben opened up his e-mail. Yes! One from Darius. Finally! About time the loser had deigned to answer.

One good thing on this god-awful day.

Wednesday

Ben piled the covers over his head, grunting when Lars stuck his head around the door and said, "I'm leaving now, but if you want a ride to the bus stop I can wait five minutes."

Ben could hear Lars breathing as he hovered in the doorway — then, exasperation evident in his tone, he said, "Suit yourself. It's raining. I'll catch up with you tonight, Ben, and no matter how much you try to avoid it, we *will* talk."

Ben didn't come out from under the covers until he heard the car engine. He was hot and sweaty, his hair sticking limply to his forehead. He brushed it aside and winced when his fingers caught the tender outlines of the weird scratches. For a brief moment, panic surged through him at the thought of school, but then, strangely, the panic was replaced by the absolute certainty that his mystery attacker would not bother him again. "Woo-woo. Cue spooky music," he muttered. "Welcome to the twilight zone! Ben the seer, who knows all and everything!"

This certainty persisted even when the first people Ben saw as he arrived at school were Baz and his cronies. They were standing just outside the gates, smoking. As he passed, Baz looked at Ben. It was hard to interpret his expression. The nearest Ben could come up with was amusement, as if Baz was privy to some huge joke on the rest of the world. He gave a mock salute and said, "All right, mate!"

"Yeah," Ben said. "I am." He carried on toward the sixth-form block, puzzled but not perturbed. Maybe his theory about the whole thing being some rite of passage wasn't so far-fetched after all.

The lower sixth common room was crowded. Even in another country, Ben could recognize the disparate tribes that made up any school. The Jocks, who colonized the area near the soft drinks machine, were muscular and fit in the latest designer sportswear. A group of Goths looked like Goths anywhere, all black clothing and lips, crouching like an unkindness of ravens by the window. Someone in the far corner of the room was waving, apparently trying to attract Ben's attention. Having first checked that there was no one behind him who was the real object of the wave, Ben hastily shoved on his glasses before he picked his way through the sprawled bodies and abandoned backpacks. As he got closer, he saw that the waver was Rob Fanshawe, the boy who had shown him around that first day. He was sitting with a couple of boys, one of whom Ben recognized from his Computer Science class. Rob shoved a pile of papers off the beaten-up sofa. "Sit down," he said. "You know Alan, and this," he said, indicating a tall, blond boy, "is Phil."

Ben had the uncomfortable feeling that he was a prize pig being shown off. All three boys were staring at him with an eagerness he found unnerving.

"So," Rob finally said, "aren't you going to tell us about it?"

Ben was puzzled, and then it clicked. "Oh, that stuff yesterday. Just some crazy kid decided to take a swing at me. I never saw him before." He resisted adding that if this was news, they must lead pathetic little lives here, softening it to "I didn't think it was such a big deal."

Phil pointed to Ben's jaw. "Looks fairly big to me, and those cuts on your forehead as well. It's been all over school this morning."

Ben surprised himself by smoothing his thick hair over the strange scratches. "Really?" Then he added, "You're right, though. My jaw hurts like hell."

"That Baz is a weird kid," Rob said, shaking his head. "No one can fathom what he's going to do next. He's always been a head case, spends a lot of his time out in the woods — poaching is what I've heard. Are you going to let him get away with it?"

Horror surged through Ben, and anger, too. Rob knew who his attacker was. Did that mean he'd been there, and done nothing to help? He stared hard at Rob. No, he'd probably just heard from someone else, but what was going on here? Rob's interest had an edge to it. Were he and his friends expecting some sort of return match? Were they after ringside seats? All three were leaning forward, anticipating his reply. "Are you guys offering to help?" he asked, grinning when they flopped back in unison and tried to look casual.

"He's a hard nut," Alan said, "but we thought a big chap like yourself might have a chance." He waved a hand as if to indicate just how tall Ben was. "Aren't you Canadians the rugged type?" he added with a touch of malice. When Ben didn't answer, Alan started humming the Monty Python lumberjack song.

"I'm a city boy," Ben said, staring levelly at Alan, who flushed slightly. "Anyway, I saw Baz this morning and he didn't give me any trouble. In fact, he was almost friendly."

Abruptly, Alan stood up to leave. "You seem to attract the weird ones, don't you, Ben? I wonder why that is? She's been asking after you this morning as well." With a jerk of his head, Alan indicated a girl sitting alone, staring openly at Ben. "Now *she* is seriously twisted!"

Ben looked at the girl, trying to work out why she seemed familiar. No girls at this school had made a particular impression on him yet. This one was small and thin, hunched forward, her arms clasped around her body, rocking slightly. Huge green eyes were fixed almost unblinkingly on Ben. A cloud of hair surrounded a face so pale it seemed to Ben that the hair was sucking all the life out of her, so bright was its red. Red hair. A flash of memory rocketed through his brain. This was the girl who had bent over him yesterday, who had said something he hadn't understood.

He almost had to force his eyes away from hers. Ben could see her lips moving, even though no one was near her. Was she repeating the words that had made no sense to him yesterday?

"C'mon, Ben, we'd better head off or we'll be late," Rob said.

Ben ignored him. "Who is that?" he asked. "She spoke to me after the fight."

"Now you've really got reason to be scared." Rob was having a hard time not laughing. "Yvonne Lea spoke to you yesterday, and today she's asking questions about you. This is a girl who speaks about once a week, and that's only if some teacher forgets that she doesn't talk and calls on her in class." Rob slapped his head in an exaggerated manner. "Oops, silly me — she does talk. She talks all the time to herself, just like she's doing now!" His face became serious. "Don't go there, Ben. Alan was teasing you, but there is something really strange about that girl. I've been at school with her since we were five and she's always been peculiar. In primary school, she had this imaginary friend. Jazriel, I think she called him. This Jazriel could do magic, had super powers. She used to threaten us with him when we teased her." Rob shuddered. "She creeps me out." He turned and headed for the door.

Ben got to his feet and slowly followed, a burning sensation on his back as if he could feel the heat of the girl's stare.

During the day Ben saw Baz a few times in the hall, but all he did was give Ben the same odd salute. Yvonne Lea was another matter. The only class they had together was English. She was waiting at the door of the classroom when he got there, and followed him in like a stray puppy. She waited until Ben took a seat and then sat directly behind him. Ben found it hard to concentrate. He knew that if he turned around, her eyes would be fixed upon him. Throughout the day, after his other classes, there she was, hovering. How the hell did she know his timetable? What did she want from him? Once or twice, Ben had thought she was going to say something, but she would abruptly turn away. It reminded him of little kids who figure that when they close their eyes they become invisible. Ben was starting to feel spooked, so he tracked down Rob who, apart from teasing him that he was being stalked, seemed halfway decent. At least in the company of someone else, Ben could ignore Yvonne more easily.

At the end of the day, Ben was forced to leave the security of Rob's company. He lived in a town house close to the school and walked home. Ben thought about wangling an invite to give Yvonne the slip and postpone the talk with Lars, but it would not be the cool thing to do. So Ben found himself walking morosely with the crowd heading toward the bus stops. Just in case Yvonne was still following him, Ben loped on down the road to the next stop. His luck held — there was no one there.

There was a seat in the bus shelter, so he flung himself down and pulled out his set text for English, Shakespeare's *A Midsummer Night's Dream*, and started to flick through it.

"He got some of it right," a small voice said. "Back then, they still knew."

Ben looked around wildly. He hadn't heard anyone approach. Yvonne Lea was huddled in the corner of the shelter staring at him.

Close up, Ben saw how thin she was. He could see the veins on the backs of her hands where she clasped the handles of a basket she was holding up like a barrier between them. He had thought her merely pale before, but now realized that it was the pallor of illness, tinged with bluish purple in circles under her eyes — beautiful eyes, with flecks of gold and warm brown floating in their green irises. They reminded him of the moss agate ring his mother had always worn, one that Lars had given to her before they were married. Ben had wanted it buried with her — it had seemed like grave robbing to take it from her finger — but his grandmother had insisted. "Keep it. Maybe give it to your wife one day." Ben shuddered, remembering how easily it had slipped from his mother's finger — the ring that she used to complain was too tight to get off. He had tried wearing it — its chunky design worked for a man or woman — but every time he had caught sight of his hand, a feeling of loss had assailed him, setting him adrift from the present. Now, the ring lay in his sock drawer, alongside Lars' cards, wrapped in an old lace handkerchief that his grandmother had given him.

Suddenly conscious that he had not responded, and noticing with alarm that while he had been lost in his thoughts Yvonne had edged closer to him, Ben asked, "Why have you been following me around all day?" He tried to speak gently, feeling that she might bolt, like a spooked horse.

"I said, he got some of it right. Didn't you hear me?" The urgency in her voice was puzzling, as if she were willing Ben to understand. She looked over her shoulder, frightened eyes scanning the empty pavement.

"I heard you. I just don't get it, that's all." Ben had had enough strange things happen in the last two days.

He didn't need some space cadet of a girl following him around and talking elliptical nonsense. "I didn't understand what you said to me yesterday, either," he said, louder and more aggressive. "So, what are you going to do? Follow me home and keep repeating yourself? Just leave me alone, okay?"

The girl's face froze, then a rush of tears coursed silently down her face. When she finally spoke, her voice was ragged. "Why don't you understand? You should understand." She repeated the phrases over and over like a weird mantra.

Ben stood up so he towered over her. She shrank away, but defiantly stared at him, mouthing the same words. "I DON'T UNDERSTAND YOU!" he bellowed. "GET LOST!"

An old woman, passing by with her dog, shot Ben a dirty look and muttered something about louts.

He bent down to pick up his backpack, ready to walk home rather than spend another minute with this crazy girl. As he was straightening up, Ben felt a light touch on his forehead. He froze, looking up at Yvonne. One of her hands was raised, almost like a priest giving a blessing.

"You should understand," she said softly, sadness evident in her face and voice. "You've been marked by one of them."

Ben opened his mouth to demand what she meant, who she was talking about, but he was stopped by the flare of panic in her eyes. She was staring over his shoulder, her mouth open in a silent scream. She turned and ran.

Ben looked back to see what had terrified her. In the distance, leaning against a garden wall, were three attenuated figures dressed in black. Ben squinted to see who they were, what was so frightening about them. He couldn't make out their faces, but their clothes were Goth. Was he in the middle of some turf war between rival cliques? The central figure took a few swaggering steps forward, clearly focused on Ben. Ben braced himself for what might come next, ready to run. The boy — Ben was sure it was a boy — stopped and dropped his hands to his hips. His movements were exaggerated and slow as he mimed drawing two guns and shooting them at Ben. Ben felt his body jerk as if the shots were real. It was only with great effort that he stopped himself from checking his sweatshirt for blood. The boy mimed blowing smoke from the ends of his imaginary guns, holstered them and touched his two fingers to his forehead in a mocking salute to Ben before he rejoined his friends. Cackling laughter rose from the group.

Ben pushed down his own anger, willing himself not to respond. There was a slight shudder and the street was empty, save for a dog peeing against the wall where the three boys had stood. "They *were* there. I saw them!" Ben muttered, hoping that the words would have the power to still his thumping heart.

Wyliff was glad that he had made the journey to the house in the darkness. The lack of trees, save for the willow in the middle of the lawn, unnerved him. The tall evergreen hedges provided a refuge, albeit an uncomfortable one. He had never been so close to a human house before, although distance was becoming more difficult as the woodlands were eaten away by building. The smells and sounds were enticing and disgusting. The house shone and hummed, making Wyliff want to run and dance wildly, but he remained rooted where he stood.

The boy had been easy to follow, although on more than one occasion Wyliff had hidden when the boy suddenly spun around as if he sensed something. The boy had heard him, too; Wyliff knew that. He had laughed when he was playing with the willow, and the boy had turned in the direction of his voice, then run off. Wyliff wondered what had scared him; he had meant no harm. Most creatures knew that. He sighed. Maybe that was the problem. Perhaps he needed to be fiercer. The boy had a fierceness about him — locked deep inside, buried under his anger and confusion. Wyliff saw it, a clear, gold glow. He coveted that fierceness. Perhaps he could make it his own when the time was right.

For Wyliff the night had gone so quickly, savoring all that was new — as if only seconds had passed until the sun rose and the house stirred into action. The man was the first to move. His hulking shoulders and thick hair reminded Wyliff of a bear. How many years had passed since he had seen a bear? Not since all the world was wood and he could roam freely. He missed bears. A bear would be a good friend to have. This man was clever, like a bear — powerful, too. Why was there such growling between the man and the boy? It was from the man that the old blood came. Wyliff saw it crackling with energy. In time, the boy would become the man. But it was the boy of now who interested him. When his skittishness faded, the boy would be a good friend, too. All Wyliff had to do was watch, wait and gently make his presence known.

Wyliff watched the boy leave, his shoulders hunched against the rain that drizzled down, before he made his move, sidling along the hedges closer to the house.

Ben pulled the hood of his sweatshirt up. It had started to rain just as he got off the bus in Cringleford — lightly at first, but now it was a constant drizzle.

He was still puzzling over what had just happened. Yvonne Lea and the three strange boys had bothered him. He had left the bus shelter and walked to where the dog was, hoping for some sign that what he had seen had been real. The dog, a mangy ratlike terrier, had bared its teeth at Ben before running off.

After that, though, Ben's luck had changed. A Cringleford bus came along. To make things even sweeter, Lars wasn't home — breathing space before the Big Talk.

Ben stopped, admiring the solidity of the cottage. He was even beginning to like the name of the place. He traced the carved sign by the door, "The Smith's Cottage," with his fingers. He'd been puzzled by that at first, and had asked Lars why it wasn't "The Parker's Cottage." Then he wished he hadn't because Lars went off on one of his rambling explanations, how old land records showed that there had once been a blacksmith living here. There was a peacefulness about it — well, there was when Lars wasn't around.

As Ben stepped to unlock the back door, he felt something crunch beneath his boot. Lying on the doorstep, one foot now crushed, was a crudely made figure of twigs and leaves. Ben's immediate reaction was one of fear and revulsion mixed with panic. For a few crazed moments, he thought that this was something to do with Yvonne Lea. She knew where he lived, and she'd got here before him and left this thing to make him recall whatever it was she was convinced he knew. Ben bent to pick it up, glancing over his shoulder to see if anyone was there. No sign of Yvonne.

He almost laughed at himself. It was like a bad horror movie. He was being haunted by a diminutive ghost.

He turned the figure over in his hands. It was the size of the average doll. Made by weaving twigs, almost braiding them, the thing's body had a hollow cagelike look. The legs and arms were cunningly fashioned so that they seemed to have joints in the right places — Ben could not work out how. The hands and feet were made from some kind of nutshells. The face, smooth and masklike, a more tightly braided basket than the body, had stuck into it two tiny brown pebbles to represent eyes. The head was crowned with some sort of brownish fiber for hair, cut or torn so that it fell over the forehead. The figure had one splash of bright color. A lime-green material had been carefully threaded to look as if the figure wore a green sweater. Ben gently touched a fingertip to the material: some sort of polar fleece. With a shudder, he realized that it was the exact color of the fleece shirt he had been wearing when he had run to the clearing, the shirt he had torn on a tree. As he turned the figure over in his hands, something rattled inside it. The ersatz sweater made it difficult to see what it was, but by holding the figure upside down, Ben was able to peer up into the hollow torso. A small stone was trapped inside. Whoever had made it must have carefully placed it there — no way could it be accidental. The stone was beautiful, golden and translucent, shot through with flecks of something that caught the light and sparkled. Amber? Ben wasn't sure, but it puzzled him. It was so deliberate that it must have meaning for the maker, but it eluded him. He carefully set the figure on the step and crouched in front of it.

His mouth was dry, his heart racing.

The figure was meant to be him. Who had made it and left it there for him to find? An awful thought occurred to him, something Lars had been droning on about primitive magic. Ben struggled to recall — something about "sympathetic magic," where a figure or doll could stand in for a person. Was that what it was? Was he going to break a foot now, just as he had broken the thing's foot?

Ben was suddenly aware that someone or something was behind him. He turned quickly, almost losing his balance as Lars loomed over him. How could he have not heard the car? Lars was staring intently at the figure where it lolled on the step. Damn, Ben thought, now there'll be questions.

"What have you got there?" Lars asked, gently reaching out to the figure with a meaty forefinger.

"Dunno," Ben replied sullenly. "It was on the step when I got home a few minutes ago." He tried to look casually disinterested.

Lars picked the thing up, his large hands surprisingly gentle, cradling its head as you would that of a baby.

"You do know it's meant to be you." He looked sideways at Ben.

"Yeah, I kind of guessed as much."

"Have you any idea why someone would leave this here? An admirer, maybe?" Lars attempted a laugh, but it sounded hollow and forced, and his eyes lost their usual smile. When he spoke again, his voice was quieter. "There's nothing more going on at school, is there, Ben?"

"Nah." Ben shook his head violently, then he exploded. "Look, Lars, the thing is creeping me out. Let's just toss it, burn it, get rid of it somehow!"

Lars' eyes widened and he shook his head. His vehement tone surprised Ben. "No. That wouldn't be a good idea. This isn't something you just dismiss. Someone is doing this and, even if you don't believe in things like this, they do. Think of it as a calling card." He held the figure up to the light and started when the small stone inside rattled. "I don't like this, Ben. I don't like it at all." Lars remained silent for a few seconds, his eyes fixed on the figure. "But I don't know what to do about it." A little laugh escaped him. "Ironic, eh? I spend my life studying folklore, so you'd think something like this …" His voice trailed away. Then he added, "Keep it safe, Ben. Promise me — if anything else like this happens, you tell me, okay?" He emphasized each word so that Ben was left in no doubt of the strength of his father's feelings.

Normally, Ben would have laughed, accused Lars of believing all that folklore crap someone was stupid enough to pay him to study and teach, but he had never seen him so serious. Lars was subdued and nervous — almost reverential. Larger than life, noisy, gregarious, overbearing — that was Lars. But this …

"Okay," Ben said automatically, but he didn't mean it. What was the point of telling Lars about the weird shit that had been happening? What could he do? Nothing. Ben shivered when taking the thing from his father — it felt as if it had settled into his hands. "I still think we should burn it, but if it means so much to you, I'll keep it safe — in my closet."

Lars remained quiet and thoughtful through dinner, barely talking. Ben thought that he might get away without the threatened talk, but once the dishes were stowed in the dishwasher that lurked incongruously behind an antique cupboard door, Lars returned to the table and very quietly asked Ben to join him.

Ben almost felt cheated, the request was so politely made. If he refused and slammed his way out, he would just look childish and petulant — so what would be new about that? He flopped down at the far end of the table from Lars and stared hard at him.

"This isn't going to be an argument, Ben. We've both proved how good we are at those. I have some things to say, and I would like you to listen. You don't have to respond, but I'd like you to hear me out, and then I'll do the same for you." He grinned then, a grin that split his beard and made him look like the young student in the few photographs Ben had found among his mother's things when he and his grandparents had cleared out the apartment. Ben had ripped those pictures into tiny pieces, taking pleasure in letting them drift from his fingers down into the toilet bowl, where they lay like scurf on the top of the water. He had barely resisted the urge to undo his fly and let rip.

"I've spent most of the day thinking — couldn't concentrate when I went down to the cathedral in Norwich and saw my first Green Man in the flesh — well, in wood and stone." Lars focused on Ben. "I was angry yesterday, Ben. I shouldn't have spoken as I did. I've said this before, and I know you don't believe it, but I'm going to say it again. It was your mother's decision that I should have little part in your life. I could have fought it, but at the time it seemed better that I didn't put us all through all the legal stuff. As to why she felt like that, I'll be the first to admit that I wasn't a very good husband, but she never gave me the chance to show whether I would be a good father. Ah!" he said when Ben tried to protest, holding up a hand, palm out, to stop him. "Let me finish. I'm not going to make excuses for how I behaved back then, but you have to realize how young we were, Ben, just nineteen, in our first year of university. We raced into marriage like it was some huge adventure. Neither of us had thought it out, beyond the fact that we were going to have fun traveling together, studying. Janine's parents did their best to persuade us not to do it, but we wouldn't listen. My dad," Lars' grin turned rueful, "knew that I never did anything he told me to, so what was the point of saying anything! Not that he was in a very strong position to give advice anyway, as this was around about the time that he left Ma and went off to Iceland to find himself! Despite what your mother may have told you, we had fun." He paused then, before adding, "For a while, anyway. Then we had to face reality. You had arrived, and traveling and studying weren't so easy anymore. Your mother wanted us to move back in with her parents, so they could help out. I wanted us to make it by ourselves. Neither of us was good at compromising. End of story." Head on one side, Lars looked at Ben. "Sad, isn't it?"

Ben looked away, not wanting Lars to see the tears that threatened. "My way or the highway!" How often had his mother ended arguments with him with that phrase?

"Shit, I'm making excuses when I said I wouldn't, Benny."

"Don't call me Benny!" Ben's growl was automatic, but it was a relief to focus on the now.

"Oops." Lars put his fingers to his mouth, looking like a parody of a mischievous kid, inviting Ben to laugh at his stupidity. "One thing that I want you to know, *Ben*, is that your grandparents love you. Never, ever doubt that. What you've got to understand is that they're old, and they're tired. Janine's illness and death took it all out of them." He looked down at his hands lying loosely on the table. "People say the worst thing that can happen is that you outlive your child."

Lars remained silent, just sitting staring at his hands, and Ben wondered whether that was all he had to say. Then Lars roused himself, shaking his head like an animal coming out of water.

"I know you're unhappy, Ben. But it's not England that's making you unhappy. You were unhappy in Winnipeg, too. And goddamn it, you've a right to be unhappy! Anyone who's been through what you have would be. I can't change that. All I can do is hope that this trip, away from places with memories, will give us time to establish some sort of relationship." Lars' voice was rising as he spoke, and he stood up abruptly, started to pace. "I'm not easy to be around. I'm loud, crude, overly dramatic, insensitive, opinionated and obsessive." He laughed. "And that's just what my friends say!"

Ben struggled to suppress the smile that threatened to undo him.

"But I mean well, Ben. Oh god, I mean well. That's what I want you to know above everything else. I may screw up, but I have your interests at heart. Please don't forget that. If you're in trouble, then I'm your man!" When Lars saw no reaction, he slumped back in his chair, put his head down and clasped his hands over the back of his neck.

Ben remained perfectly still. He tried to work out what he felt, but it was too hard. He knew that, unless he got out of the kitchen fast, he would start to cry or yell.

He stood up from the table quietly, carefully pushing in his chair and opening the door. Then, in a voice that sounded as if it had belonged to someone else, said, "I've listened like you asked, Lars, but I'd like to go to my room now."

Lars neither looked up nor said anything.

Pulling the door closed behind him, Ben took several steps up the stairs, then flopped down. He hadn't switched on the hall light, welcoming the dark that now surrounded him. He couldn't take it — not this measured quietness. It was much easier to hate someone who was red-faced and roaring with anger, who wouldn't listen, who only thought of himself — the Lars his mother described. Ben had learned early on not to mention his father, not to ask questions about him. When he forgot, his mother told Ben the same stories, even using the same words to delineate

Lars' inadequacy and explain how the failure of their marriage was his fault and his alone. It was the only thing about which she had argued with her parents. Ben remembered the yelling, the period of not talking that had followed his grandfather's mild suggestion that maybe Ben's mother and Lars had just been too young to marry.

Thursday

Ben drew his knees up and rested his forehead on them. It didn't help. His head still ached. His eyes felt swollen and heavy. He had half expected Lars to come bounding in this morning, his usual bellowing self, demanding to know what Ben had to say. But he hadn't. Ben had heard the car leave a while ago.

A while ago! Ben reared up and lunged for his alarm clock. Shit! He'd forgotten to set it. It was almost nine. He was going to be late. Ben hastily grabbed clothes, hoping that they were only creased and not actually dirty. He grabbed his backpack from where he had thrown it in the corner, then stopped suddenly. The twig figure was sitting next to it. That couldn't be. He was sure he had put it in the closet.

"I don't have time for this craziness," he muttered and went pelting down the stairs, flying out the door just as the cleaning lady drew up in the driveway.

"Can't stop. I'm late," Ben yelled and ran full tilt to the main road, only to see the bus pulling away. "Shit! Shit, and double shit!"

When Ben finally made it to school, it was nearly ten. The first period was over. He had no idea what to do, just sidle in or report to the office. In the end, he settled for sidling in, hoping he was too new for anyone to notice his absence. It helped that it was break. The halls were packed, so he did not stand out. As he made his way to the common room, Ben became conscious of someone walking closer than was comfortable; he could almost feel breathing on his back. He spun round, fists bunched, half expecting to see Baz. It was Yvonne. She cowered, but stood her ground.

Before Ben could speak, she put out her hand, as if to touch his forehead again, but drew it back at the last second. "You saw them, didn't you?" Her voice was quiet, flat. She didn't meet Ben's eyes, but stared past him, her gaze flickering around as if she were on guard.

"I saw three boys. Yeah, what of it?" It was there again, the feeling of compulsion that Ben felt when Yvonne stared at him. He couldn't work out whether she did have some weird power or just that she was so pathetic and lost that he felt sorry for her.

"They're not boys." Yvonne was shaking her head. "Not boys," she repeated.

Fighting back the urge to laugh, Ben said, "Boys, young men, whatever! They didn't seem particularly friendly and they obviously scared the shit out of you, but, hey, stay out of their way. If that doesn't work, go to the police."

"He wants me." Yvonne's eyes were rolling now, and Ben thought that she was going to have some kind of fit.

He couldn't help it — he laughed. The idea of Yvonne as lust object was just too funny.

Ben's laughter seemed to focus Yvonne. She looked directly at him for the first time. Her eyes brimmed with tears. He stumbled over his words, trying to talk away the guilt. "Look, I'm sorry I laughed, but it's all a bit bizarre, you have to admit. Why are you telling me this? Haven't you got some girlfriend you can talk to?"

"I had no friends but him." Yvonne stopped, gulping down a sob. "I thought he was my friend, but he's changed. He's going to come for me, I know. He wants to use me." The sobs were coming hard now. "He says that I have the sight, the old blood."

People were starting to stare. Ben edged a little away from Yvonne, shifted his backpack so that he held it in front of him. She was crazy, gabbling nonsense. "But why tell me? Do you have some wild idea that I can help you?"

"Yes!" Yvonne's face lit up. "You can." She smiled, and Ben realized how pretty she might be if she weren't so scrawny and haggard. "One of the old ones has marked you. He wouldn't do that unless you had power. You saw. No one but me sees them. That means you're like me. That means you can help me." Her desperation tugged at Ben, but revolted him, too.

"No!" He held up his backpack as if to ward Yvonne off. "This is all bullshit. I can't do anything for you."

Ben took off running, not looking back until he reached the safety of the computer lab. He dropped down into a seat, ignoring the curious glances. Rob Fanshawe leaned over. "You all right?" Ben just nodded and focused on the screen.

Losing himself in the clean language of programming helped. It was hard at first, but gradually his whole attention became so absorbed by the problem he was working on that he was slow to react to the commotion outside the lab's door and the approaching wails of sirens. En masse, the students spilled out into the hall, ignoring their teachers' protests.

Ben shouldered his way to the front of the crowd.

With Mr. Greengrass crouched at her side, Yvonne lay on her back. Her eyes were open, but appeared to see nothing. Her body and limbs were rigid, shaken by slight tremors.

Bile flooded Ben's mouth. "What happened?" he asked the person standing next to him. He reared back in shock when he saw that it was Baz, the familiar knowing smile on his face.

"You mean you don't know?" Baz asked, his eyes glittering and hard.

A girl, standing on the other side of Baz, chimed in.

"She was standing outside the door, like she was waiting for someone, when she like just collapsed."

Ben directed his next comments to her, ignoring Baz, who still smiled at him. "Did anyone do anything to her?"

"No," she said, as if Ben was accusing her of something. "I already told you. She just collapsed. There were people around, for sure. Some stayed. Someone went and got Greengrass." Then, as if she had just remembered something, she added, "Just before she fell, she held up her hands, like she was warding someone off and pushing them away, but there was no one there. She is seriously weird." The girl shuddered and turned away.

A chill ran through Ben, but before he could ask anything more, paramedics with a gurney pushed their way through the crowd. They worked efficiently, and it seemed only seconds before Yvonne's rigid form was wheeled off with Mr. Greengrass in attendance.

Something had happened.

Wyliff's whole world had shivered. He was unable to move, limbs locked in spasm, senses straining. Leaves were stilled as the breeze died. A rabbit stood petrified in mid-lollop. No sound came to his ears. He wanted to howl his anguish to the tops of the trees, but his voice was trapped inside.

When it ended, it was as sudden as it had come. A great rushing roared through Wyliff's head. The leaves in his hair and beard flattened against his skull and chin. The creepers around his legs and arms relaxed and he fell in an ungainly heap to the ground. The rabbit darted off, but Wyliff could sense it hiding, quivery, in the brush. Birdsong filled his ears, warning calls, shrill and piercing, as the birds hovered uneasily.

The boy would not come tonight, but it would be soon. He would wait. Waiting was something Wyliff was good at. He stood, shaking himself out, hearing the rustle of foliage. A tall oak beckoned. Wyliff loped over to it, pressed his body against the solid trunk, felt the kinship of its sap whispering its song of age through the tree.

He shut his eyes and waited.

Yvonne Lea's dramatic collapse was the sole topic of conversation for the rest of the morning. It seemed everyone had a story of the girl's odd behavior and general weirdness. Ben couldn't stop himself listening. He felt almost responsible somehow for her collapse. Three times — wasn't three a significant number? — she had sought him out, convinced that he could help her, citing ties binding them; three times he had rejected her. As people vied to come up with the best Crazy Yvonne story, he wondered if there was something in what she'd being saying. He'd seen weird things, too. In a couple of weeks, would they be talking about him like this? Okay, the girl was strange — even if half the stuff people were saying was true, she was definitely not normal. A loner, talking only to herself, with gestures and facial expressions — not the way to win friends, for sure, but there was a mean-spirited glee in the stories, and that bothered him. He had found her scary, but pathetic, too. Maybe it was because she looked as if a breeze would blow her away like dandelion fluff, or maybe it was her terrified frustration when Ben hadn't understood her at the bus stop. Maybe it was even the helpless fear that he had sensed when she had seen the dark trio. Whatever it was, Ben wanted to defend her. He had stuttered out something a couple of times, but no one would listen, preferring their version of Yvonne. Gradually, other topics of conversation took over and Ben couldn't make up his mind which was worse — the jibes about Yvonne or the indifference. In the end, he mooched off down the hall, thinking that he should have stuck with keeping to himself.

The hall was full of people heading to the cafeteria or out into the grounds. Ben turned to find a quiet place in the library when he spotted Mr. Greengrass, walking head down, shoulders hunched. It was like a jolt of electricity — he must have just come back from the hospital. Ben sped up to catch him. The teacher glanced at him and then slowed down, a worried look on his face. "Ben, is everything all right?"

Why was Greengrass asking him that? He was the

one with the questions. Ben kept walking, avoiding Greengrass's concerned look. "Yeah, fine. I just wondered," he hesitated, unsure how to go on, unsure whether he wanted to go on. The words finally tumbled out in a rush. "That girl, the one who got taken away in the ambulance this morning. Is she going to be all right?" He didn't look up.

"The girl?" Mr. Greengrass sounded puzzled. "Which girl would that be, Ben?" His face was blank.

Ben felt as if he was teetering on the edge of some dark chasm. He stared hard at Greengrass, trying to work out if this was some cruel joke. "The girl who fainted. The one you went to the hospital with." He was conscious that his voice was louder than it should be.

Mr. Greengrass shuddered, his face twisting into an expression that Ben found hard to recognize, as if he was fighting for control. "Oh," he said, "you mean Yvonne." He paused, shook his head ruefully. "That is so odd. How could I forget that?" He stood there, silent.

"How is ... she?" Ben demanded, having difficulty saying her name.

"Her grandmother came," Mr. Greengrass said. "Yes, that's right. Her grandmother came and I left."

He started to walk away.

Grabbing his arm, Ben persisted. "But how is she?" People were looking at them now.

As if unaware of Ben's grip on his arm, Mr. Greengrass continued almost conversationally, "You're the only person who's asked me about Yvonne, Ben. Now that's odd, don't you think? Are you friends, then?"

"No!" Ben shouted, "but I'm scared for her." The funny thing, Ben realized, was that he *was* scared — more scared than he had ever been before. His fingers dropped nervelessly from Greengrass's arm.

Mr. Greengrass's blank face twitched. His eyes closed briefly. When they reopened, they looked different. Ben couldn't help staring — the color was odd, not gray, but a kind of weird lilac. When he spoke, there was a strange timbre to his voice, an almost metallic edge. "You should be, Ben Larsson! Oh, how you should be!"

Ben flinched as the teacher reached toward him, but all Greengrass did was pat him on the arm and, in his normal voice, say, "She's in some sort of coma, Ben. The doctors were puzzled by it, even asked me if she took drugs." He laughed then. "No, not Yvonne, I told them. Well, it was nice that you asked," he said dismissively, surveying the crowd around the cafeteria door before he moved off.

It was some minutes before Ben could bring himself to move. He had no power in his legs. He was aware of people moving around him, parting like he was a boulder in a river. He glanced at his watch. It was 1:00 PM. He had twenty minutes before his next class — ah, screw it, he thought. He had already missed one period today, why not make it two? Lars probably wouldn't be back until early evening, so he could have the house to himself and e-mail his friends back in Toronto, not that any of them were good correspondents. Yeah, why not just walk out?

No one stopped Ben as he made his way out, but he thought that it would be stupid to wait at the bus stop in front of the school, so he decided to walk for a while.

The sun was shining, yet there was still a damp chill in the air. English weather, he thought, and wished that he hadn't dashed out of the cottage without a jacket. The broad Newmarket road toward Cringleford had little traffic. Ben walked past the large houses that crouched solidly behind their hedges, trying to stop his mind from straying to Yvonne Lea and Mr. Greengrass's bizarre behavior. He was a firm believer that if you ignored something, it might just go away. His mother's way of dealing with things. Like a flare of pain in a decayed tooth, the thought flashed through Ben. Don't go there, he thought desperately.

Confused half thoughts and feelings fought in Ben's brain. He saw the strained look on his mother's face, heard the determinedly casual tone in which she told him that she had a doctor's appointment — his mother who avoided going to doctors like the plague. That one appointment becoming a series of urgent hospital visits, then stays. There was the sharp, otherworld smell of hyacinths in a blue pottery bowl sitting on the windowsill of the specialist's office, the distant rumble of the man's voice as he explained to Ben and his mother that if she had only come when she had first found the lump in her breast, there might have been more that they could do.

A sudden rush of wind buffeted Ben, bringing him back. He had reached Eaton, the village before Cringleford. He walked down its tiny main street, forcing himself to look into the shop windows, although there was nothing to interest him there. Once over the humpbacked bridge, the houses were smaller, closely packed together along Intwood Road. When he hit Keswick Road the trees began to take over, the houses hiding behind them. The lane to the group of cottages was a dirt track with no sidewalk. Ben concentrated on avoiding the potholes, allowing no other thoughts to intrude. He was dimly aware of movement among the trees on the right, a flicker caught at the corner of his eye, but when he turned there was nothing there.

"You're scaring yourself!" he said out loud. Ben tried a laugh, but it sounded false and forced. All the same, he was glad when he was out of the tree-lined tunnel and onto the open area in front of the cottages, where the sun finally seemed warming. There were no cars, but no one was ever around during the day. Lars said it was ironic that what had once been farm laborers' cottages were now all owned by rich professional types, who either used them as weekend getaways or worked in Norwich. Wait — there should have been a car! When he had left this morning, the cleaner had been arriving. She was paid to put in a whole day, and it was only early afternoon.

The front door was open. Ben stepped cautiously in. Dried leaves crunched beneath his feet, obviously blown in from outside. A bucket full of soapy water and a mop stood in the doorway to the kitchen. Ben bent down and stuck a finger in the water. It was cold. The kitchen was spotless, but a quick run through the house showed that the rest was as they had left it. Back in the kitchen, he could hear a muted electronic mutter. Finally spotting the telephone receiver off the hook and lying on the countertop, he replaced it and noticed, weighted down by the salt shaker, a piece of paper.

Sorry, had to go early. My granddaughter's been in some kind of accident. Taken to hospital. I'll make up the time.
S. Lea

Why had he not made the connection before? Sure, Lea was a common name, but he should have caught the similarities between her and Yvonne: both were small and thin, and Mrs. Lea's rusty gray hair must once have been as red as her granddaughter's.

A flash of blue caught Ben's eye. Lying on the countertop was a feather, and next to that some acorns. Puzzled, he picked them up, feeling their smoothness. The feather could have blown in, but the acorns … Ben spun round, but there was no one there. He ran awkwardly into the hallway, throwing open the doorway to the small living room. Satisfied that it was empty, he went up the stairs, two at a time. Ben felt a slight pang of guilt as he opened Lars' door. The piles of books by the bed looked unsteady as usual. A heap of clothes under the window caused his heart to skip a beat, their bunched shape looking like something crouched there. The tiny bathroom was empty. His own room was the only one left. Ben hesitated, trying to remember whether he had shut the door that morning. It was open now. Everything looked normal: the unmade bed he'd scrambled out of in such a hurry, his sleek black computer — Lars' guilt gift bought on the day they arrived in Norwich — on the table under the window. Ben mentally inventoried the room's contents. Then he saw it. Lying on the pillow was the strange figure that he had found. But it was not alone. Next to it was the picture of Ben and his mother that normally sat by the computer. One twiggy arm had been arranged so that it looked as if the figure was pointing at Ben. Ben flew across the room, grabbed the picture, desperately trying to avoid any contact with the thing. He hugged the photograph tightly to his chest and then stopped, unsure of his next move. Someone had been in the house, that was obvious, but who and why? Was it Mrs. Lea playing games? Was she as strange as her granddaughter? Abruptly, Ben turned and ran down the stairs. He couldn't make up his mind whether he was more scared or annoyed — but he didn't want to be in the house right now. He grabbed his backpack, stuffed the photograph inside and left, making sure the door locked behind him.

Everything was quiet. In the distance, Ben could hear the faint rumble of cars on the bypass the other side of the woods. "Shit! Where the hell do I go now?" The long hike back into Norwich was unappealing. He cursed his own stubbornness. Lars had wanted to buy him one of those little motorbikes that English boys seemed to like so much, but Ben had always found excuses not to try one out.

"It'd give you some independence" was all Lars had said, shaking his head.

If only he had given in, Ben would have been able to take off now, just head down the road, away from all the things that were messing up his life and freaking him out. A giggle escaped him — his long frame hunched over a moped was hardly Easy Rider.

It could be as much as three hours before Lars got home. Making a sudden decision, he shouldered his backpack and set off for the clearing he'd found. He'd prop himself up against one of the trees and read. At least he'd be prepared for English class tomorrow.

Wyliff was looking for things he could use to lay a trail to bring the boy to him. So far, he had acorns, toadstools and feathers — crow feathers that shone blue black. He had found them, lots of them, scattered under an oak tree. The birds had been fighting, that he sensed, and not just the usual scuffle over territory. This had been a melee with many birds involved. He spread the feathers out like a fan in front of his face, sniffing at them as if this would tell him just how disordered things had become. The wrongness was a constant pulse. Wyliff shivered.

"No!" he said. "Not yet." This had been a long time in its coming, hours or days would make no difference. He needed time to tease and trick the boy until he was open to his approach. Night would be best. Moonlight made it easier.

Wyliff stiffened. Someone was close by. He could hear the grass squeak as it was walked upon. How could he have been so careless? Too much to think about, too much to do. He flattened himself against his refuge, the oak, feeling himself almost sink into its bark. It took all his will to remain still, to calm the quivering leaves, the tightening vines, as the boy burst into the clearing.

The boy was carrying a bag. The object of power in it, the one that the boy clung to. Wyliff felt a tremor run through him. It was the key, that he knew, the key that would secure the boy's help.

Ben looked cautiously around. He had thought that leaving the house would free him of his uneasiness, but it was turning into fear. He felt the frame of his mother's picture through the soft canvas of his backpack, let his fingers trace it and then hold on firmly. He thought back to the day it had been taken. They had gone to spend the weekend in Muskoka at her friend Bob's cottage. Ben had been bored, and he sensed that Bob didn't really want him there, but he had gone along to keep the peace. Ben's mouth twitched in a smile — his mother somehow always got her way. Bob had wanted a weekend alone with her, and Ben preferred staying in Toronto with his grandparents. But she had won out, and there they all were. It hadn't turned out too badly — Ben had discovered that Bob loved science fiction, and there was a whole stack of old *Analog* magazines that Ben had devoured. That gave his mother and Bob time alone, and they had taken the canoe out for hours. The picture had been taken when they came back from one of those outings. They had been gone longer than Ben had anticipated, and he had started to worry. He had been waiting down on the dock, and as soon as his mother clambered out of the canoe, she had hugged him, a fierce, hard hug. She always had the uncanny knack of knowing just how he was feeling. Bob had snapped several pictures without them knowing. Ben loved this one. It showed him bending slightly, pulled down by his mother's embrace. His eyes were shut, but he was smiling, his mother's cheek against his, her face almost beatific.

Ben sighed, holding the backpack tight against his chest. It was a week later that everything turned to shit, that his mother went to see the doctor. How could she still look so happy? This was what he found so hard to understand: she knew something was wrong, but did nothing, didn't give him a chance to do anything. Ben felt the familiar twist inside, the sorrow entwined with a rage that he dare not let loose. He concentrated on deciding where to sit. Reading would be safe.

Wyliff relaxed as the boy's eyes passed over him, unseeing. Relaxed so much that he was taken by surprise when the boy plopped himself down at the foot of the oak tree and rested his back against Wyliff's legs.

He bellowed. He couldn't help it. The touch was so alien, so powerful. The echoes of his sound reverberated around the clearing, and he struggled free of both the tree and the boy, and then froze, horrified at what he had done.

Ben was thrown roughly to the ground, as if the tree had shuddered. A sound was forcing itself into his head, a shout, but also a powerful wind.

Then he saw him.

Standing stock still by the oak was an impossibly tall creature. Humanoid in general outline, its edges were softened by leaves and vines that twined around its elongated limbs. Two terrified eyes peered out of a mask of leaves that covered the head like a helmet before bushing out into what appeared to be very much like a beard. The creature was holding up one hand, as if to ward Ben off. Its mouth hung open as the awful sound continued to buffet Ben's ears.

Ben scrambled to his feet. His heart felt as if it was going to explode. He took a hesitant step toward the creature, knowing in an instant that it meant him no harm, that it was as scared as he was.

The creature backed away. "No!" it said, "not yet," in a voice that rustled and boomed. Then it turned and ran, ungainly, as if its joints were stiff.

Ben was not aware of time passing.

"Not yet" replayed in his head. Strangely calm, he flopped down on the leafy mulch, sifting it with his fingers, bringing it to his nose to smell its damp, vegetative odor. Whatever the thing had been, it should have scared him — scared him shitless. It was impossible; it couldn't exist. Yet he had seen it, felt it. Even heard it. What was worse was it was familiar. How had he instinctively known that it was harmless? No, it wasn't harmless, it was dangerous. But it *meant* him no harm. There was a difference. He felt as if he had been plugged into a circuit board, as if new information, a new reality was being formed around him in which everything was connecting, but which he had yet to understand.

Somewhere in the wood an animal screamed. There was a commotion in the undergrowth, and a rabbit burst into the clearing, its eyes wide and staring. No sunlight forced its way through the leaves. Shadows were growing. Where had the afternoon gone? Unless he hurried, Ben would have to make the last part of his way back to the cottage in darkness, and that was something he wanted to avoid.

Friday

Ben's whole being was concentrated on not thinking, not remembering. He had spent too much time today thinking, worrying until he felt panic-stricken. He doggedly hiked up Colney Lane, focusing, walking as fast as he could, looking at the houses, even counting their windows, anything to block out what had happened yesterday.

The solid houses soon gave way to fields, and Ben walked along the side of the road, kicking up clods of earth. Seeing the squat brick buildings of the agricultural research facility, he knew that he had not much farther to go. Within minutes the road barriers appeared and the hospital loomed over him — a monstrous pinkish-gray castle of a building that glittered in the late afternoon sun. Where the bloody hell was the entrance?

Ben decided that the surest way was to pretend he was a car. He trudged along the side of the main road, ignoring the cars that shot past, some of them honking. At a roundabout, a blast of signs assaulted him. Wards

— that would do it, he thought, and sure enough, he soon found himself in an entrance hall. Hospitals smelled the same the world over — a sharp, antiseptic smell that couldn't disguise the sweet, rotting odor of illness. A sudden spasm racked Ben's gut and he struggled to control the flood of memories threatening to overwhelm him.

He tried to win back the calm he had felt after the encounter with the strange creature yesterday — there had been no fear then, just the feeling that he was part of an elaborate cycle of events over which he had no control. In fact, it was the normal that had begun to feel bizarre. By the time he had got home from the woods, Lars was there and had started supper. Ben had grunted answers to Lars' comments and questions about Mrs. Lea's sudden departure. If anything, their conversation had remained civil a little longer than usual. Dinner was over before Ben stomped out accusing Lars of prying when he had asked him how his day at school went. It was a fabrication, though, because Ben knew that if he had stayed he would have been tempted to tell Lars what he had seen in the woods. He shook his head, trying to remember the evening after that. Nothing. Today was clear, though. It had been business as usual, dull lessons, reverting to keeping as low a profile as possible. No one mentioned Yvonne. He had even asked a girl in their English class about her, but she had just looked blank.

When he repeated the question, her face had closed in, her eyes skittering from Ben's face. "Yvonne?" she asked. "I don't know anyone called Yvonne." He hadn't pressed, just repeated the experiment on others, with the same result. He seemed to be the only one who had any memory of a waifish girl called Yvonne Lea. Even their English teacher, Mr. Haslett, had denied knowledge of such a pupil. Ben had lingered after the lesson and approached him as he packed his bulging briefcase with the essays he had just collected from the class. He had looked up at Ben quizzically. "No, don't tell me. You've been here only a couple of days and already you want to give me pressing reasons why you haven't handed your work in?"

His overacting had caught Ben off guard and he had found himself smiling. "No, I've done it. It's in."

Haslett had affected an exaggerated Norfolk accent. "So, bor, yew want to tell me to go easy on you, because yew're just a por colonial who can't make head nor tail of us here yokels!"

"No, no." Ben had struggled not to laugh. He had forced himself to be serious. "I just wondered if any of the teachers had heard how Yvonne is?"

The change was instantaneous. Mr. Haslett's face had stiffened, the smile vanishing. "Who's she, Ben? I think you've got muddled up. Perhaps she's in one of your other courses. I've not got anyone called Yvonne in this class. Sorry, don't know who you might mean." With that, he had picked up his briefcase and swept out of the room.

It was then that Ben knew. He wasn't mad. There was a girl called Yvonne Lea. She had the crazy idea that he could help her, and now she was ill. He felt he owed her, especially as she seemed to have been magically erased from everyone else's memory. As soon as school had ended, Ben had set out for the hospital.

He looked around the lobby. Several people tricked out in burgundy waistcoats were hovering. One, an older woman, caught his eye and stumped over. "Can I help you?"

Stuttering, Ben blurted, "A friend of mine was brought here yesterday. I was hoping to see her. Could you tell me which ward she's in? Yvonne Lea?"

The professional smile didn't waver, and the words had been said many times. "The receptionist over there will help you. Have a nice day!"

Right! Nice day? He was sweating, the clammy sweat he remembered from the hours he had spent by his mother's bedside. Why were hospitals always so damn hot?

The receptionist hardly looked up as Ben said Yvonne's name. Ben felt despair seeping in — what if the hospital had been struck by the same amnesia that had magically descended on the school?

The receptionist, fingers flying over the keyboard, named a ward. "Yep, she's here." Ben quickly headed for the bank of elevators, ignoring the receptionist's pointed "You're very welcome." He didn't have time for social niceties.

His luck held. The ward sister directed him to the far end of the six-bed room. Sitting on a hard chair was Mrs. Lea, holding Yvonne's hand on the puke-green coverlet. She looked up at Ben as he hovered awkwardly, her expression unreadable.

Ben started to stutter out how he wanted to see how Yvonne was doing, but her grandmother cut him off with a wave of her hand.

"You don't have to explain. She told me she'd met you. She said you might be able to help." Mrs. Lea looked at him hard. "I didn't know what she meant by that, but one never did with Yvonne." The older woman's face crumpled. "Does, I mean. Does, not did."

Ben couldn't meet her eyes, couldn't handle the naked need in them. This wasn't a good idea. He looked longingly over his shoulder toward the door.

"Bring a chair over and sit down." The old woman's voice made disobedience impossible.

Once he was settled, Ben was at a loss. What the hell could he say — that no one at school cared or even seemed to know that Yvonne existed, that weird things were happening and that Ben had the feeling, although he had no evidence, that Yvonne was the focal point of it all? He stared down at his hands, but kept sneaking glances at the figure lying motionless on the bed, so small and slight that she hardly raised the covers.

Yvonne was on her back, her long, red hair fanned out on the pillow around her, as if she were resting on a pillow of blood. Her bone-white face was expressionless, the eyes closed. Ben shuddered — his mother had been like that at the end, only she had been surrounded by beeping machines, not just the single IV going into the back of Yvonne's hand. There was another difference: one that chilled him. Once the drugs had taken effect, his mother's face had been expressionless because it was slack. Yvonne's face held a strange tension, a rigidity that reminded him of the carved faces of the saints in the churches that Lars had dragged him to see. In fact, the closer he looked at Yvonne, the more unreal she seemed. He found himself checking to see if she was breathing.

Forcing himself to straighten up, Ben became aware of how closely Mrs. Lea was scrutinizing him. "Do they know what's wrong?" he asked. Her eyes were a curious shade of reddish brown. They reminded him of the rabbit he had seen in the woods.

She shook her head. "They run all sorts of tests, pricking and poking at her, but nothing. All them doctors say is that the test results are normal, but they don't know why. She hasn't stirred since they brought her in." She flicked at the IV tube with a disdainful finger. "That's to keep her fluids up. If she doesn't wake soon, they'll have to feed her through that, too." In a sudden, darting movement, she reached out and grabbed Ben's sleeve. "What did she say to you? Do you know why she's like this?" Shaking him, she hissed, "You can help her, can't you? That's why you're here, isn't it?"

"No!" Ben's voice was louder than he intended.

Some of the other patients glared at him. One visitor tsk-tsked loudly. "This is a hospital. Have some respect."

Dropping his voice, Ben continued, "I mean, I'd like to help, but I don't know how I can. I came because I felt sorry for her. No one else seemed to care."

Letting go of Ben's arm, Mrs. Lea bridled, a look on her face that was suspiciously close to triumph. "That's typical, that is. They never have bloody cared. If they had, maybe she wouldn't have had to spend so much time alone, mooning around in the woods by herself."

Ben felt as if he had been jolted with an electric shock. "The woods?"

Mrs. Lea looked at him as if he were mad. "The woods at the back of yours." She snorted. "Not that there's much left of them now, not with all them new houses being built near the bypass." She added, when Ben looked puzzled, "We live on Keswick Road, me and Yvonne ... she's been with me ever since her mum ran off to London when Yvonne was four. Good riddance, I say!" She sighed. "Poor little Yvonne didn't think so — she cried every night for a year and was always hanging around outside, waiting for her mum to come back. Fair got on my nerves, I can tell you. I was glad when she took herself off into the woods, especially when she told me she was playing with friends there. Full of them she was. She'd come back, smiling and telling me all about what they'd got up to." Mrs. Lea's face changed, darkened with anger. "Should have realized it was all a load of nonsense, that she was making it up — Jaz, Fitch, Quoil. Who gives children names like that? Not even the posh people who live where you do would be that daft." She grinned then, a sly little grin, watching to see whether her jab found its mark.

The woods. It all came back to the woods. Ben felt restless, confined by the antiseptic smells, by Mrs. Lea's need. "I've got to go," he said abruptly and stood up.

"But you didn't answer me," Mrs. Lea almost wailed. "What did she say to you? Why did she speak to you?"

"I don't know. I couldn't make sense of it. Something about the play we were studying." Ben could feel anger rising now. "I'm sorry she's ill, but I can't do anything about it. I shouldn't have come here." He was shouting now. "Just leave me alone, okay?" he yelled at Mrs. Lea, who half stood as if to prevent him leaving. He rushed from the ward, almost knocking over a nurse coming hotfoot to see what all the commotion was about.

"Fuck it! Just fuck it!" Tears were blinding Ben. He wanted out, away from sick people and monitors and IVs. He knew people were staring, but he didn't care — all that mattered was getting away.

The sun had disappeared behind low clouds by the time Ben negotiated his way back through the concrete maze of the hospital entrance. Colney Lane was quiet, with few cars passing by. He sucked in huge gulps of air, his sides aching. A copse in the distance caught his eye. Although there was no wind, the trees swayed and seemed to writhe. Ben ran.

The harsh tones of a car horn stopped him. In amazement, Ben realized that he was on Church Farm Lane, almost home. He was covered in sweat. His legs ached and there was a dull throb just above his kidneys where his backpack had been bouncing as he ran.

"Race ya?" Lars' broad, beaming face peered out from his ridiculous car. He didn't wait for an answer. "Jeez, Ben, I didn't realize it was you at first. I've never even seen you move at a fast walk, let alone run flat out."

Too winded to talk, Ben shook his head and flopped down in the seat next to Lars.

It seemed like only seconds before they pulled up in front of the cottage. Ben's ragged breathing was easing.

"Thought it was going to rain, trying to outrun it." Lame, he thought, very lame, but Lars nodded, a look of relief settling on his face.

"Those clouds do look ominous," Lars said with a jerk of his head to the left.

Ben was stunned to see a wall of cloud behind the cottage, so purplish black they made the sky seem bruised.

May his roots shrivel and die! May his fruit rot and corrupt on the stem! No! Not that one. Wyliff's knobby fingers covered his mouth, as if he could force his words back into being unsaid. Why, why had the man come just then in the green thing? Wyliff had it planned. While the boy's mind was lost in the rhythm of running, this would have been a good time to approach him, to tell him what was needed. Now he would have to wait.

He pressed deeper into the woods, watching lights come on in the house. The man and boy were apart, one low, one high. The man was moving, moving, light glinting on things almost hidden in his huge hands. Wyliff shivered. Wayland the Smith had hands like that, hands that were powerful and dangerous, hands that worked and changed things. Their old blood was the blood of Wayland. They were changers, both. Back in the long ago, one of Wayland's smithies had been here. It was fitting that those with his blood had come here. It was meant. With a start, he realized that the boy was standing at one of the house's many eyes, looking out toward where Wyliff stood. Could he see him? Was it something simpler — a sense of him, perhaps? Maybe the fetch was working. Wyliff grinned. The fetch was not as cunning as he would have liked — there had not been time — but it had power. He had watched when the boy had found it, knowing that once he touched it a connection had been made. He had not liked the way the boy had hidden it inside a dark hole. It had taken much, but Wyliff had pulled at it with his mind, forcing life into its limbs until it rested with the image that hurt and drove the boy.

Wyliff turned as heavy drops of rain began to bombard him. This was an unnatural rain. It had been made. The clouds had come too quickly. Their colors were wrong. Was it a warning or a challenge? Wyliff did not know. But the game had been set in motion, and soon it would be his move.

"Ben, don't go crazy on me, but I know something's up." Lars raised a hand as if to forestall an outraged protest, then looked shocked when Ben said nothing. "It's more than the usual crap between us. In fact, for once, I truly do believe that it's nothing to do with me at all." He leaned forward over his plate, trying to see Ben's expression. "Is it school? Do you hate it? Are you being given a hard time? Is it that little punk who laid into you?" Lars' face was getting red, his fists were bunched.

"I'll come there, sort it out once and for all." Lars consciously unclenched his hands, spread them out on the table on either side of his plate. "Is it to do with that thing we found on the doorstep? It's called a fetch, by the way." Lars hesitated as if not sure how to go on. "Look, I know some teenagers like to experiment, play around with Ouija boards and the like, dabble in what they call magic. If you've got in with a crowd like that, just tell me." Lars subsided into silence, impaled on the withering stare that Ben fixed him with.

"Sure, Lars." Ben drawled the words. "Good thinking. I've been at the goddamn school less than a week. I haven't made one single friend, let alone infiltrated the school's coven!" He was pleased that Lars was unable to meet his eyes, that he colored slightly in embarrassment.

Lars started up again, taking a deep breath. "Look, if you really hate the school," he paused, as if it was difficult to say the words, "you don't have to go. You can have a sabbatical, too. It's not a big deal. All it means is that when we get back to Canada, you'll graduate a year later. Or you could take some correspondence courses, work at your own pace on the Internet. And we can still get you that moped. You could maybe explore a bit of the countryside. Anything, if it would make you happier." Lars' voice had a pleading note to it, but he had recovered himself enough to stare hard at Ben as if willing him to open up.

Ben felt very tired. He had mechanically shoveled down the food that Lars had made, aware that his body ached with hunger. He could hear what Lars was saying, hear the concern, but didn't know how to respond. What could he say? "I think I'm being haunted by a creature that's half tree, half man. I'm seeing people who vanish. The teachers and kids at school are suffering from collective amnesia about a girl called Yvonne Lea who's been a student there for the last six years and some have known all their lives. Someone or something is leaving stuff for me to find, like they're setting a trap for me or a puzzle that only I can solve." He knew how crazy it all sounded and tried to find something that he could say, something that would get Lars off his back.

"Lars." The word dropped unbidden from his mouth. A rush of panic followed. Was he going to spill his guts? Breathing slowly, Ben started again. "Lars, don't sweat it. It's not that bad at school." He saw relief erase the lines of worry around Lars' eyes.

"But something *is* bothering you?" Lars was looking at him shrewdly. "Something's happened in the last couple of days." He gave a forced laugh. "I mean, it's not like you're usually a ray of sunshine, but you've been moodier than ever. Something, or maybe someone —," Lars' appraisal of Ben intensified as he watched to see the effect of his words "— is getting to you."

Shit! Nothing got past Lars. Nothing his mother had ever said gave any hint that Lars was this intuitive. "An oaf!" she had usually called him.

His mind weighed what to say next. "Look, it's no big deal, okay? A girl at school had some kind of fit. It was scary — ambulance, the whole deal. She's in my English class, but I just know her to see her. Only, she's our Mrs. Lea's granddaughter. That's why the old woman took off on us the other day." Lars was looking thoughtful, but Ben felt that he was not satisfied. "It bothered me ... a lot." Hanging his head, he tried to assess whether playing the guilt card would get Lars to leave him alone. When he saw Lars about to speak, he went on, "Okay, Lars, I did something really stupid. No one else seemed to give a shit, not even the goddamn teachers, so this afternoon — when you caught up with me — I was coming from the hospital. Someone had to see how she was." Ben's shudder was involuntary. "It was a mistake. I got freaked — the whole hospital thing. That's why I was running like that." Even as he spoke, Ben wanted to take the words back; they took him to a time that he didn't want Lars to share, that Lars had no right to share.

Instead of the barrage of questions, the rough sympathy Ben was expecting, even an invitation to talk more, all Lars said was, "Yeah, I can see that. I get that." Lars pushed his chair back and went to the fridge, returning with a bowl of fruit salad that he plunked down in the middle of the table. "The girl," he asked, "how is she? Is there anything we can do?"

Ben wanted to laugh. Lars was trying so hard, not crowding, avoiding the subject he wanted to talk about. It was pathetic, but kind of funny, too. He imagined Lars rushing from the room, running to his bedroom, sticking his head under the covers and letting rip with all he really wanted to say, a flood of questions and opinions. His smile misled Lars.

"She's going to be okay?" Lars asked hopefully.

"They don't know what's wrong with her. She had some kind of fit, and now she's in a coma. Her grandmother's a wreck."

"Shit!" Lars' reaction was heartfelt. "Poor old woman. I'll call and tell her not to worry about here. We can manage, eh?" He didn't wait for an answer, spooned a vast serving of fruit salad into a bowl. As he ate, he stared into the middle distance.

Ben stared out the window. He liked the view over the garden and into the woods. With no houses behind them, and no lights, it was easy to imagine what it must have been like here long ago. The back of Ben's neck prickled. There was something out there, he knew that — something looking in at him, even though he could not see it. Something that wanted, no, it *needed* him. It was the creature he had seen the day before.

Ben stood up abruptly. "I'm going for a walk." He heard but ignored Lars' protests about it being too late, that it would get dark soon, that he had homework to do, that it was still raining slightly. It was only when Lars told him to wait — he'd come as soon as he finished his fruit — that Ben shouted, "No! I don't want you to come with me. Why would I want to be with you?" He turned fast, not wanting to see the pain in Lars' eyes, and went out the kitchen door.

Ben put as much distance as he could between himself and the cottage. A quick glance over his shoulder confirmed that he was safe — Lars was not following him. Ben could see his bulk backlit at the window. He was glad that the shadows hid Lars' face.

At the edge of the woods, Ben hesitated. He was not sure why he had to go for a walk. He never went for walks. And Lars wasn't even giving him a hard time. Tonight's dinner had been one of the most amicable times they had spent together, even though it was killing Lars to have to hold his tongue. Power, Ben thought, what power I have! He cackled evilly, then laughed again, louder, when the echo of the first laugh came back at him. This time there was no echo, just a velvet blanket of silence and night. Ben felt all his senses heighten. He knew now why he had come out. He was coming to meet someone.

Listening to the reverberations of his mirror laugh, Wyliff waited. The boy had to come to him. That was the way it had to be. Ever since the man's arrival had thwarted him, he had been thinking of the boy, strong thoughts that would call him. Now his reward had come. The boy was standing at the edge of Wyliff's domain. A minute would bring him to the clearing where Wyliff stood — not seeking succor with the oak, but centered in his own skin. Wyliff knew that others were abroad tonight, too, but they were occupied, not aware of what he was doing. This was good. They thought him impotent, part of the old world they sought to remold to their own fancy. He started to sway, a gentle rocking like that of a sapling. It calmed him.

"Hoooah!" he let out his breath in one powerful exhalation. The boy was on the move.

Ben liked the woods at night. The moon was full and it silvered branches, making it easy to find his way to the clearing. "I should be scared shitless," he muttered. "I'm losing my marbles!" Ben giggled. "And I don't give a damn!"

The boy was talking. Was this a greeting? Wyliff tried to form words, but none came. He moved toward the boy, raised a hand.

"Fuck!" Ben had forgotten how big the thing was. Eight feet, maybe even nine feet tall, it towered over him, one arm raised. He couldn't help it, he dropped, curled into a ball, his arms protecting his head. What felt like twigs pulled at his clothes, plucked at his arms. Ben sensed great power held under tight control. He allowed himself to be gently raised up.

The creature had crouched down, legs bent at what seemed odd angles, alongside him. Its breath gusted into his face, breath that smelled of wind, rain and leaves. Russet eyes regarded him solemnly. Ben stared back, fascinated — the eyes had no whites. Why didn't it say something? Why did it just stare, with a need in its eyes? Ben surprised himself by reaching out and touching the leaf mask that covered the creature's upper face, snatching his hand back when the leaves shivered and the creature flinched.

"I'm sorry. I didn't mean to hurt you! Did I hurt you?"

The creature's words when they finally came were in a voice so filled with creaks and rustles that Ben had to strain to understand. "I am not hurt, but your touch feels strange. If it is what you want, I will bear it." This was said with such pained resignation that Ben almost laughed.

He closed his eyes and shook his head. This was so bizarre. Surely he would open his eyes and find himself back in bed — the whole thing a nightmare. When he opened his eyes, nothing had changed. He was still standing in the wood next to something that could not exist, yet he saw it, felt its breath, had touched it. "What the hell are you?" The words burst out of him.

"I am Wyliff and you are the boy."

"A Wyliff? What's that?" Even as he asked, Ben knew that he had made a mistake, that he was being given the gift of the creature's name.

"I am Wyliff and you are the boy." A glint of amusement sparked in the creature's eyes and his beard of leaves quirked upward.

"Wyliff is your name, right? Yeah, I'm a boy, but I have a name, too. I'm Ben." Ben moved away slightly, wanting breathing space, thinking space even. The creature — no, Wyliff, Ben thought, don't call it The Creature like something out of a bad horror movie — scooted over until his back was against the trunk of the largest oak that ringed the clearing. He sat with his knees up, long arms wrapped around them. Ben smiled as he realized that Wyliff was aping his own favorite way of sitting.

"You've been following me and watching me, haven't you?" Ben knew the answer, knew it deep inside, but needed to say it out loud, if only to help make all that had happened have some logic, however twisted and surreal. "You left that thing on the doorstop." Ben felt his innards twist at the thought of the little figure that seemed to move at will around his room. "Why?"

Wyliff looked steadily at him, refusing to be hurried by Ben's vehemence. His answer, when it finally came, a whistling whisper like the wind in winter, surprised Ben. "I need your anger."

"What kind of garbage is that?" Ben was shouting, spittle flying. "Everyone's angry, not just me." He paced around the clearing, whacking the underbrush with a stick, blind to Wyliff's wince every time the stick connected. "Why me? Lars has a serious temper. Why not him, eh?"

Wyliff said nothing, but brought his chin down to rest on what passed for knees.

"I'm sick of it, okay? Everyone is always telling me that I'm angry." The words were pouring like hot vomit from Ben. "My grandparents, Lars, even that asshole psychiatrist they sent me to see last summer." Ben screwed up his face, his voice unctuous and false. "Now, Ben, it's okay for someone who's been through what you have to be angry. It's natural. But you have to deal with your anger, you have to work through it. Then you can let it go." Ben stopped. His face shone in the moonlight, awash with tears and snot. "I don't *want* to let it go. If I do — she goes, too!" Ben looked down at the stick, which he had snapped in two. His voice was quieter now, but still raw. "Sometimes when I think about her, the only face I remember is the empty one, when she was lying in that shitty hospital bed, dying. I try to see her alive, like when she and I would go to the movies — it was so weird, she loved action films, car chases, explosions — but I can't." Ben shook his head and looked up as if just remembering where he was and to whom he was talking. "Ah, shit, what's the use? You probably don't even know what a goddamn movie is, do you?"

Wyliff creaked to his feet. His face cracked wide in a gleeful smile. "This is the anger I need," he said. "An anger that burns. An anger that hurts. An anger that gives power. An anger that is cherished. An anger that wants to save."

Ben's mouth dropped open in astonishment. Then he laughed so hard that by the time he stopped, he was gasping for breath.

When he finally had enough breath back to speak, Ben looked up at Wyliff. "Not exactly sentimental, are you? Bit of a single-minded bastard, eh? So tell me then, what do you need my anger for, and who or what the fuck are you?"

"I am Wyliff and ..."

"Yeah, you said already." Ben flopped down at the base of the oak, looking up at Wyliff until he gingerly lowered himself next to him, amidst much rustling of leaves and vines. "But there's all kinds of weird shit happening. Are you doing that?"

"No!" the answer was a bellow of outrage that stretched Wyliff's mouth into what looked like a scream. "I want it to stop. I want *you* to stop it."

Ben sighed. This was hard work. "Stop what? And how? I've seen people vanish in front of my eyes. Someone is in a mystery coma, and it's like she's been erased from everyone's minds except mine and her grandmother's. And there's ... you." He waved a hand weakly at Wyliff as if this gesture could encompass the strangeness of talking to someone who seemed both man and plant.

If he thought Wyliff would be offended, Ben got a shock. Wyliff's leaves were erect and trembling, his eyes wide and staring. His twiglike fingers clenched and unclenched convulsively. "Look," Ben said, "I'm sorry, but you're a little strange, okay?"

"Taken!" the word came out like the rasp of branch on branch. "They have taken someone." Wyliff took a huge gulp of air, as his toes seemed to extend and burrow into the earth. He didn't speak for several minutes, just breathed heavily, his eyes closed. Gradually, calm returned and he was completely still. "The court turns," he said. "Jazriel has had his way. Seelie becomes unseelie."

"Who's Jazriel?" Ben demanded. "Wait, I've heard that name before."

Wyliff surged to his feet, dragging Ben with him, one hand lifting him with ease. "Who has been taken?" he demanded. Ben's feet scrabbled for purchase, but Wyliff held him above the ground. He pulled at his sweatshirt where Wyliff's grip bunched it tight against his throat.

"Goddamn it, you're hurting me!" he yelled. "Let go!"

Wyliff's fingers opened and Ben fell to the ground.

"It is worse than I thought, so much worse," Wyliff keened. "What are they planning? Who have they taken?"

"There's a girl." Ben struggled to think what he could say that would have meaning for this strange, wild creature. "A girl from my school, a girl who lives near here." He wasn't sure that this was the right answer, but he had the gut feeling that Wyliff's shock, his distress, began when he had described Yvonne in a coma.

In a voice that rose and fell, Wyliff said, "A red-haired girl. A girl who has the sight. A girl who has the old blood like you. A lonely girl. A girl who loves these woods."

Ben blanched. Everything was connecting. Who had taken her and why? He tried asking those questions, but Wyliff rocked backward and forth, chanting his description of Yvonne over and over.

"Ben! Ben!" Ben could hear Lars lumbering through the trees from the cottage. "Ben, where the hell are you? It's nearly midnight!"

With a last glance at Wyliff, Ben headed in the direction of his father's voice. "I'm coming!" He shouted to cover his panic. He did not want Lars to see Wyliff — would he be able to see him? And how could it be nearly midnight? Time seemed to have no meaning for Wyliff. He would still be there in the clearing tomorrow.

Ben picked up speed and jogged toward home.

Saturday

Ben woke feeling as if metal balls were rocketing around inside his skull. He sat up groggily, surprised to find himself still in his clothes from the night before. A twig was pricking his hand, a hand that was crisscrossed with scratches and scrapes. "Aaagh." The groan was clotted and full of phlegm. He gave an experimental cough and felt a little better. At least it was the weekend.

His room was gloomy, even though his clock read 10:00 AM. Wincing as his neck cracked, Ben tottered over to the window. It was streaming with rain. Brushing his hair back from his forehead, Ben's fingers snagged against the carved letter scab.

Wyliff! He had to get back to the clearing. If only Lars hadn't come crashing in last night … Ben sighed. Okay, Lars was concerned — he had been out for hours — but did he have to make such a drama out of it?

"I was that close to calling the police." Lars had shoved his thumb and forefinger in front of Ben's face. "I didn't know whether to stay here or look for you. What the hell were you doing all that time?" His eyes had narrowed. "Do you meet someone in those woods? Back home I could hardly get you to leave the house. Here, you've suddenly become nature boy."

"I've told you — I don't know anyone here. All my friends are in Toronto." Ben enjoyed the way he could call on his anger to blaze so easily.

"Okay, " Lars had yelled back. "So, what the hell were you doing then?"

"Thinking." Ben had kept his voice neutral.

"Thinking for five hours! So, have you solved all the world's problems then? Didn't you realize how worried I would be?" Lars' face had gone almost purple with rage. "You could have fallen, broken a leg. I know this is a quiet place, but who knows what psychos hang around the woods?"

Ben had laughed then. He hadn't meant to, but he was picturing Lars' face if he had seen Wyliff. The laughter had sent Lars over the edge, into full rant: he was sick of Ben's attitude, tired of trying and trying and hitting a blank wall. He had loomed menacingly over Ben, but Ben had let it wash over him, closing his ears and mind, turning his thoughts to Wyliff.

A silence that he sensed had lasted for a while brought him out of his reverie.

"Well?" Lars had roared. "Don't you have anything to say to me?"

In his politest voice, Ben had said, "I'm tired. I think

I would like to go to bed now." He had maneuvered past his father and out of the kitchen. He had heard rather than seen Lars' fist thump against the wooden door, slamming it behind his back.

He had expected to lie awake, his nerves jangled by all that he had seen, by the row with Lars, but sleep had fallen on him as soon as he had sat on the bed.

As Ben clattered down the stairs, he was struck by how quiet the house was. Glancing through the fan light on the front door, he saw that the car was gone.

A plate, mug and frying pan were in the rack on the draining board, and the smell of bacon hung in the air, but the teapot was cold against Ben's hand. Ben grinned as he saw the dent in the chipboard door. He bet Lars was nursing sore knuckles this morning. A note, riddled with translucent grease stains, was anchored by the butter dish.

> GONE INTO THE CITY. WILL BE BACK AT SUPPERTIME. MAKE SURE YOU ARE HERE THEN.
> LARS

I might be, I might not, Ben thought defiantly. Snagging a banana and a granola bar from the pantry, he loped out through the back door and across the garden.

The leaves dripped on him. The ferocity of the rain had already caused some to fall, and Ben noticed that their green was being replaced by browns and reds. He could smell woodsmoke, and it took him back to the cottage of his mother's friend, Rob, where they had spent Thanksgiving the last few years. No. Not last year. His mind veered away, not wanting to think about it.

Ben braced himself for the possibility that he might find the clearing empty, but there was no need. Wyliff stood in the middle of it. The leaves around his mouth rustled as if his hidden lips were moving, but there was no sound. His eyes were open but saw nothing — he did not react when Ben stood right in front of him.

Ben took the time to look long and hard at Wyliff, without the shock of their first meeting or the cloak of night. Ben could now see how easy it would be for Wyliff to lose himself among trees, despite his size. His skin, the little that was visible between the leaves and vines that twined over his tall frame, was the color of bark, rough with small cracks and fissures, some greened with a delicate fuzz of moss. Rain made the skin slick and glossy. It was around Wyliff's head that the oaklike leaves were most abundant. Although Ben had seen them move and knew that they were a growing part of Wyliff, they looked like a close-fitting mask from brow to mouth, out of which peered his large eyes. The leaves on Wyliff's face were tinged with encroaching autumn, but Ben doubted that they would fall. Above and below the leaf mask, green tendrils, intertwined with sprigs of acorns and berries, mimicked what would have been human hair and a beard. A small movement at the top of Wyliff's head startled Ben, only to reveal itself to be a tiny wren that looked quizzically down at him.

Tired of Wyliff's immobility, Ben jumped up and down, waving his arms and calling his name, but Wyliff remained locked deep in a trance. Feeling like a child being ignored by adults, Ben gently touched his hand, causing Wyliff to shiver. His eyes scanned the clearing as if looking for a threat. When all had been examined, Wyliff turned his gaze on Ben.

"You came back." It was a statement, but the alien voice shocked Ben anew.

"Damn right, and I want some answers. Now." Ben was trying to sound authoritative, but Wyliff's steady gaze and massive presence made him feel that he was indulging in useless posturing. Wyliff would reveal only what he wanted to, and only what would make Ben do whatever it was that Wyliff wanted.

A tiny smile played around Wyliff's lips. "I have been thinking," he said. "I have thought long and hard of what you told me, boy."

"Don't call me boy. My name is Ben."

"Ben." The name sounded clipped and hard when Wyliff repeated it. "Ben," he said again, almost as if he were tasting the word, mouthing it like a bone. "We will sit and I will answer some questions. Others have no answers save what you must see." Wyliff crashed down onto his knees on the wet ground and waited for Ben to follow suit.

Ben wished that he had thought to bring a coat with him, but he was already drenched. With a sigh, he flopped down, talking as he did so. "Okay, you're still not saying anything, just sounding mysterious. I don't need that. I want to know who you are, or what you are, and why you've picked on me."

"I am Wyliff."

"Oh, for christ's sake, you keep saying that. Who is Wyliff?" Ben could feel anger flaring inside him corrosively.

"Wyliff is who I am." This was delivered in a sing-song cadence, as if the words had been said many times. "And here is where I have been for ever and always, from the time when all the world was woods until now, when the woods wane. I am the woods, and the woods are me. Once the woods were many and there were many mes; now the woods are small and there is only me." Wyliff looked at Ben as if this all made perfect sense, and, in a funny sort of way, it did.

Ben felt like laughing. "If only Lars knew, all that folklore shit that he's been studying for years — that stuff that I think he half believes — it's actually true!" He shook his head, a flare of memory lancing through his brain — the cover of a book that Lars treated like a bible. "No! This is too much. You're a fucking Green Man, aren't you? A guardian of the natural world, fertility symbol — all that." He clutched his sides, wanting to hold in the irony of it all.

Wyliff smiled in return. "I am Wyliff!" he said in a triumphant, ringing tone, and Ben knew that he was right.

"Okay, okay," he said, "enough already with the 'I am Wyliff' stuff. I know who you are and I think I know what you are now, but why have you been following me?" Ben jabbed an angry finger at Wyliff. "And you made that image of me, didn't you?" He pushed back his hair from his forehead. "This, too!"

Wyliff lay one knobby finger gently on Ben's chest. "First, I marked you as mine. Then, I called you. You have the anger, the fierceness, the old blood."

Ben pounced on the words. "Old blood — that's what you said about Yvonne. But she and I are not related."

Wyliff rose stiffly to his feet, long limbs cracking as they straightened. "I tire of talking."

"Nooo," Ben wailed, like a child whose favorite toy has been snatched away. Obviously Wyliff's behavior was not governed by any rules that Ben understood.

"The court is on the move. Seelie becomes unseelie. Jazriel has his way. I will show you. Tonight when the darkness is here." Wyliff strode off, his long legs crossing the clearing in two steps.

"Do I come here?"

"Willow" was all the answer he got, and he found himself alone in the clearing, his soaked clothes clinging to his skin as he shivered, teeth chattering.

A long soak in a hot bath had gone some way to warm Ben up. Now he sat at the kitchen table, a steaming bowl of leftover stew in front of him. He savored the rich flavor and sighed, thinking that whatever his failings might be, Lars was a much better cook than his mother. She threw together wieners with a side of Kraft Dinner or brought home takeout. She used to joke that all the fast-food restaurants near their downtown condo had named her customer of the week. Suddenly, Ben pushed his bowl away. He was no longer hungry. Reaching forward, he pulled toward him the books that he had liberated from Lars' bedroom. He looked at the one that had helped him to recognize Wyliff. *A Little Book of the Green Man*.

What was it that had caused him to make the intuitive leap that this was what he was dealing with in Wyliff? The cover picture, a bearded man with branches issuing from his mouth, looked nothing like him. It was only when he flipped the book over that it hit him — stylized though it was, the carving, with its oak leaves and acorns surrounding staring eyes, was definitely Wyliff. Green Men were Lars' particular obsession, and he'd heard him yammering on enough about them to have an idea of what they were supposed to be. He sighed, remembering a particularly boring dinner given by Lars' boss as a farewell — they had talked about how Green Men could be equated with woodwose or wild men. But now, having seen what those stuffy fools only dreamed about, he got it.

Wyliff was maddening, but he had a vitality, both threat and promise, that drew Ben. He didn't see it all yet, but he knew that Wyliff was a living embodiment of the natural world, and that something was wrong with that world. It was more than the encroachment of buildings whittling away the woods and open spaces. The balance was fundamentally threatened, and Yvonne's strange coma was a manifestation of that. Ben sighed. Yvonne's still form haunted him. It took all his willpower not to see it every time he closed his eyes. But it was strange — although he felt scared and unsettled, he also felt alive for the first time in months. He knew that Wyliff was manipulating him, but he also had the sense that he could do something to make things better. And, to his surprise, that mattered a lot.

Ben turned the book over in his hands. It was so small that it could fit in his pocket. Would Lars notice if he borrowed it? What sort of reaction might he get from Wyliff if he showed it to him? Nah, he thought, Lars would notice.

The other book was larger, *An Encyclopedia of Fairies.* Ben figured it would be a good one, if only because its pages were well thumbed, some drifting free of the spine. He tried looking up "Green Men," but there was no entry. He flicked forward to the w's, trying "wild men" first, and then, when he had no luck, "woodwose." A brief article didn't tell him much that he hadn't already picked up: woodwose/wild men were supernatural creatures living in woods, covered in hair just as Green Men were covered in leaves. He continued reading. "Yes!" "… often to be found among the carvings in East Anglian churches." Well, where the hell were Norwich and Cringleford if not in East Anglia!

Ben searched quickly for the other names Wyliff had used. He was in luck, both "seelie" and "unseelie" were there. They referred to fairies, or fairy hosts or courts. Fairies! Without warning a vision of Disney's Tinkerbell swam into view — a little cartoon with gauzy wings. A giggle burbled up inside him. "Clap your hands if you believe in fairies!" Maybe not. Turning pages quickly, Ben went to the entry for "fairy," sucking in his breath as he followed what the author was saying — how fairies, or fey, as they were more properly known, were a whole range of supernatural beings both benign and malignant — seelie and unseelie! A feeling of triumph flashed through him. Would his luck hold? He raced to find an entry for "Jazriel." Nothing. Nada. Zilch.

"What's this?" Lars' voice made him jump. How could he have not heard the car, or the door opening?

"Following in my footsteps?"

Ben bit back the "You wish!" that sprang to his lips and said, "Nah, just looking up stuff for English — *A Midsummer Night's Dream* — borrowed some of your books, okay?"

Lars nodded. "No problemo!" But he gave Ben a searching look, before theatrically hitting his forehead with the heel of his hand. "Hey," he said, as if suddenly struck by an idea. "How about we go eat at the pub down in Eaton, the old one over the bridge, and then go to the movies in Norwich?"

Ben winced. Wyliff had muttered mysteriously about darkness. It got dark about 8:00 PM — did he mean then or later? He realized it was irrelevant. Wyliff would wait. He needed Ben. And Lars was staring at him like a giant puppy. "Why not?" he said, trying to sound as bored as possible. "There's fuck all else to do around here."

A full moon illuminated the garden. Ben sat in the dark by his window, his eyes fixed on the willow. It stood there, just a tree. He sighed, but did not turn away. As soon as they had got back from the movies, Ben had excused himself, saying that he was tired and had some schoolwork to do. Lars had not protested, just nodded, and patted Ben roughly on the back.

"That wasn't so bad, was it?" he'd said.

Ben had seen the hope in his father's eyes. "It was okay," he said, keeping his voice noncommittal. He now realized that it *had* been all right. Lars had been in fine form in the pub, but not too over the top, giving Ben a running commentary on the various English types he spotted. Even the movie had been fine, once Ben had dissuaded Lars from the latest *Terminator*. Too many memories with a film like that — not that Lars would know that. The comedy that was the only other bearable thing on offer had made them both laugh and, for stretches of time, Ben had been able to lose himself in it.

Something rattled against the windowpane. Corny, Ben thought, the old tossed-pebbles routine. But the garden was still empty. The noise came again: not pebbles, sticks. Like a small dust devil, wind was whirling sticks up against the window. Ben could not see Wyliff anywhere, but he decided to go down and wait by the willow. He picked up the backpack, which he'd emptied of school stuff and packed with a flashlight and a waterproof jacket. It was close to eleven — with luck, Lars was asleep. He'd heard him creak up the stairs almost an hour ago. If Lars followed his usual pattern, he would have read for only about twenty minutes. Peering around his door, Ben let out a silent sigh of relief — no light coming from Lars' room, only heavy snores.

Remembering which steps creaked was difficult, but Ben made it safely down, hearing no interruption in Lars' resonant rumbling. Ben had a sense that the cottage was alive in a way that it was not in the daytime, that it was aware of him, waiting for something.

Ben ran to the willow. Strangely, there was no wind now, and the willow's long branches hung still, forming a cage. How had the twigs been whirled up in that mini-tornado?

Wyliff was not there. Resisting the urge to swear, Ben forced his way through the branches and threw himself down on the ground to wait as long as it took.

"Aaagh!" A cry of pain came from alongside him, causing Ben to jump up, his eyes searching wildly for its source. His backpack, which he had tossed down, suddenly flew back at him, the flashlight inside clunking hard against his left shin.

"Shit!" Ben found himself staring into a small, bearded and furious face.

"Don't you be swearing at me, bor!" The voice was surprisingly deep, its accent strongly Norfolk. "You threw the pouch first, hit me roight on me 'ead. Bloody human!" The last epithet was said with a pugnacious thrust of the chin. A small figure stepped forward, fists clenched and raised.

Ben fought back laughter. "I'm sorry," he said. "I really didn't know anyone was there."

The little man seemed somewhat mollified by the apology. He sniffed and lowered his fists. "Tha's humans all over, never do see anything other than their own big ugly selves!" He looked Ben over. "And you're bigger an' uglier than most!" he crowed, slapping his sides as he laughed. "Wyliff, he told me about you, see, but he didn't say that." The smile dropped. "Not that he ever does say much. Just moons around being mysterious and commooning with trees. Normally doesn't talk to anyone, strange old Tree Man, especially not to the likes of an humble hob like the poor old Billy Blind!"

Ben's mouth was open, ready to ask questions, when Billy Blind, for he presumed that was the creature's name, stuck out one hand and said, "Come on, then. Time's a-wasting! Wyliff said I was to wait for you and bring you, so let's get moving."

When Ben did not move, Billy Blind stamped his booted foot, grabbed Ben's hand and yanked with surprising strength.

Ben let out a squeak of fear, thinking that he was being pulled head first into the trunk of the willow, but his head never connected with wood. Instead, he felt himself being stretched somehow, and the world blurred around him.

"Come on, you great lump. Get up off your arse!"

Ben found himself sitting on the ground among some trees, overlooking an area of heath. Heath? Where the hell could they be? No heath land in Cringleford.

"You hanging on like a dead weight threw me sense of place. Wyliff's a ways off. It's just as easy to walk now." Without waiting to see if Ben was following, Billy Blind stumped away, muttering and grumbling to himself, something that involved a lot of swearing and the word "human."

Resisting the temptation to look around, Ben hurried to catch up with his guide, who threaded his way deftly through the trees. Billy Blind. The name had a nice alliterative ring to it, Ben thought, and he couldn't imagine calling him anything but that. He definitely wasn't a Billy, and Mr. Blind sounded ridiculous. He had said he was a hob, whatever the hell that was. Hobgoblins he knew, for sure, and the hobbits that Tolkien wrote about, but the little man in front of him was different. If he had been standing still, Billy Blind would have come up to midthigh on Ben, but he appeared shorter because of his sturdy breadth. He was wearing rough woolen pants tucked into soft leather boots. A sleeveless jerkin of what looked like sheepskin added to his overall bulk. Thick, grayish white curls covered his head and spilled down over his collar. Slung over his shoulders was an assortment of pouches that bulged with odd shapes and bounced as he kept up a steady, stumping pace that Ben found hard to match.

When Billy Blind finally came to a halt, Ben was out of breath — which seemed to amuse the little man.

"Oi, Leaf-face! I've bin and done what you asked. Can I bugger off home now?" Billy Blind's voice was low but piercing.

A rustling of leaves was the only answer, and then Wyliff detached himself from the majestic oak by which Ben had been standing. He just stared down hard at Billy Blind, who fiddled with the largest of his pouches, withdrawing a knife and a small piece of wood. When Wyliff flinched, Billy Blind looked up slyly and said, "Hold you hard, it's from a dead branch I found on the ground. Didn't hurt one of your precious trees, did I?" He concentrated on whittling the twig, but muttered as to himself, while wanting Ben and Wyliff to hear him. "Doesn't matter if the Billy Blind is inconvenienced does it, dragged away from his nice, quiet home, oh no? Not when the high and mighty are concerned. Have you ever spoken to me before, Leaf-face? Not bloody likely. Only now you've got yourself all in a tizzy about something, then I'm your new best mate, and it's the good old Billy Blind to the rescue, doing the dirty work, having to consort with the great, lummoxy human boy I've managed to avoid for the month he's been living near my home. Thank you, now that would have been nice, but maybe that would be too much to expect."

Ben listened, fascinated — here was a master at grumbling — so that the hundreds of questions that fizzed inside him remained unasked. When he started to speak, it was too late. Wyliff grabbed his shoulder and spun him around so he faced the heath, with a hissed "They come!"

At first, Ben couldn't see anything, even though Wyliff's long arm was extended in a quivering point to the far side of the heath. The moon had gone behind a cloud and all was darkness. It was only when he realized that a patch denser than the rest was moving that Ben was able to make out what so bothered Wyliff. Billy Blind had let the knife drop from his hand as he stared, too.

It was a procession that marched majestically out of the trees and onto the heath. Faint strains of music drifted on the still night air: sweet horns and lutes, but these were interspersed with raucous blasts of rock music, rap and techno. The figures in the procession were all dressed in silks and furs, though some looked moth-eaten and tattered, ranging from a silvery white to a deep black with the sheen of a raven's wing. As faces drew closer, he saw that it was only a few older ones who were in white — many more wore shades of gray. The young were garbed in black leather, some stylized to look like the carapaces of exotic insects. Some walked, others rode horses. Two were on the backs of giant hounds — one white hound with blood-red ears, the other a huge black dog whose fur seemed to absorb all light around it. The sight of these two beasts drew a shudder and susurration of breath from Wyliff.

"Seelie becomes unseelie."

"Blood and lights," Billy Blind chimed in. "I never knew they had turned so much. There's even a god-forsaken Gabriel hound there, and Shuck, Black Shuck," he said, pointing to the dogs. "If they've teamed up with Herne the Hunter, then you're done for, Tree Man."

Ben was torn between disbelief and awe. He had never seen anything like these people. These must be the fairies, the fey from Lars' book. He was aware of Billy Blind maneuvering around him to get closer to Wyliff, but paid little attention to the hob, instead drinking in the magical sight unfolding. Its strange beauty stirred something in him — an otherworldliness that held promise, escape.

"Where's their king? Where's Havriel?" Billy Blind was whispering urgently to Wyliff. "He wouldn't be putting up with this unseelie nonsense. And listen — that's tuneless human music. He wouldn't be having that, either. Havriel insists that the Fey keep to themselves, preserve what's left to them, now that there's bloody humans everywhere." Billy Blind aimed a kick at Ben, grinning wickedly when it connected. "Wyliff, where is Havriel?" Billy Blind's voice was sounding querulous now, even scared.

"Jazriel has his way," Wyliff answered simply. As on cue, a vast cacophony of sound ripped through the quiet night air, with human music battering the quieter Fey lutes and horns. The procession froze.

Out of the trees raced three motorbikes dragging trailers. Two flanked the frozen troop of Fey, but the middle one drove straight at it. Ben drew in his breath, waiting to see long bodies fly through the air, fall like broken birds. Just as the robes of those in the back row were being stirred by the motorcycle nearing, the group parted, silently and without looking at the rider that swept through their ranks. Forming an arrowhead, with the middle bike as the point, the machines roared across the heath toward the woods, cutting up the grass, filling the air with the stench of their exhausts. Horror burned through Ben — the riders were the three boys who had menaced Yvonne at the bus stop, the ones who had disappeared. But the trailers held greater horror.

In the trailer on the left lay the still, stiff figure of an old man on a bed of dirty sacking. He was bound from chin to toes with what looked like sticky spiderwebs, like some vast cocoon. His pale features were clammy and beaded with sweat, his dark gray eyes burning with impotent fury.

Ben had to look away, but was drawn to the trailer on the right. Instead of the smooth path followed by the others, the rider was struggling to prevent his machine from fishtailing erratically as the trailer's passenger capered wildly, bouncing off the sides and gibbering like an ape. As the bike approached the trees, the figure slowed its dance and turned knowing brown eyes on Ben, Wyliff and Billy Blind. It gave a little nod, and Ben saw the mouth move, the lips forming a familiar phrase, the one he had heard Baz use the day after the fight. "All right, mate!" He shuddered.

But the worst was still to come.

The three bikes slewed to a halt some ten feet from the trees. Wyliff was immobile, leaning back toward the oak; even Billy Blind was still, crouched low to the ground, the earthen colors he wore making him appear like a small boulder. Only his brown eyes showed life — and a measure of fear. Feeling very exposed, Ben concentrated on not moving anything but his eyes, trying to see who or what was in the final trailer. The middle rider sat proudly in his saddle. Black hair with a greenish patina to it was pulled straight back and up, forming a thick horsetail flowing from the top of his head. Bone-white skin covered sharp, angular features like a bird of prey, the only color the blood-red, wide slash of his mouth, and eyes that burned with violet fire.

With exaggerated movements, the rider stepped off his machine, allowing Ben and the others a view of the trailer.

Yvonne.

Enthroned — that was the only way Ben could describe her — on a dark crystalline chair shot through its depths with flashes of vermilion and green fire. It looked to Ben as if it would hurt to sit on such a chair. Yvonne's gown floated around her like misty gray cobwebs. Her long, wavy hair was loose, its red vivid against the dark that surrounded her. A circlet rested on the top of her head, rather like a crown. The circlet was made of rose briars, and the same thorns edged the bodice of the dress instead of lace, small pinpricks of blood marking their presence. But it was her face that made him lose control, cry out her name.

It was the icy, rigid face he had seen in the hospital, but that face had been something unreal. Now he saw the real Yvonne, held captive. The rigidity was born of tension; she was fighting something with all her strength. The muscles in her thin neck were corded, and veins stood out like blue worms. Beads of sweat clung to her skin. Her eyes behind paper-thin blue lids twitched. Her lips were moving, but no words came out.

Ben felt rather than heard Wyliff speak, a soft breeze of words. "Jazriel has his way." The sound galvanized him into action. He lurched forward, intent on snatching Yvonne free, not thinking how, not caring what it might cost him, but he found himself unable to move. No matter how hard he willed his muscles to work, nothing happened. His voice was frozen, too.

"Control your dog!" The voice was pleasant in timbre, but cruel in its delivery. "I should not have to do it for you, Green Man."

Wyliff stepped slowly forward, so that he stood alongside Ben. The rider took a small step back as Wyliff peered down at him. Billy Blind uncurled himself from the ground, edging closer to Wyliff.

"Jazriel." Wyliff's voice was flat, muffled — an acknowledgment, nothing more.

Jazriel turned and grinned at his two companions. "Have you come to watch our triumph, Wyliff? The first steps of our transformation, when we shuck off the old ways." He cast a contemptuous glance at the bound figure in the trailer.

"Unseelie harms. It takes pleasure in pain." Wyliff took another step forward, but this time Jazriel did not fall back.

"Oh, that it does," he said quietly, struggling not to laugh, "but what power it brings, what new experiences." He flicked a finger first at Baz, for now Ben saw that it was indeed Baz in the right-hand trailer, and then at Yvonne. "Aren't humans delicious? So vital and inventive. We always avoided them, and what have we got for it?" His voice was now rising to a scream that shattered the night air. "Nothing but loss — loss of place and, because of that, loss of our power." As if suddenly conscious of being out of control, Jazriel took a deep breath and attempted a laugh. "Look at what poor, pale shadows we have become." He spat on the ground. "Humans, they're everywhere! So now we must change. We will seek them out, use their things, feed on their power, live in their world!" He looked directly at Yvonne, who stared blankly back. "She will beget the future." His face soured. "When she stops foolishly resisting us."

His smile returned only when he sauntered toward Baz. "Some are not foolish," he said. "Some seek us out." Baz was still as the tall Fey approached. His eyes glittered, and there was an eagerness in his expression that Ben could not interpret. Baz reached out his hand to Jazriel, who took it and held it hard.

Baz's limbs jerked uncontrollably. His eyes rolled back in their sockets, spittle dripped from his slack mouth. Only Jazriel's grip on his hand prevented him from falling.

A luminescent glow bathed Jazriel, flaring in rhythm with Baz's twitches. Finally, the Fey let go, almost pushing Baz from him. Baz collapsed in a tangle of loose limbs on the trailer bed. Ben could hear his ragged panting, as if he had been running for miles.

Jazriel put both arms above his head, stretching lazily, like a contented cat. "A little crude," he said, "but powerful. When the human comes to, he will get his reward. He is not very much harmed." Jazriel smiled at Wyliff. "You have your dog," he said, pointing to Ben, "and I have mine. Mine will be a hunter dog, bringing me others, and you will watch my power grow, Tree Man!"

"No." Wyliff was shaking, leaves trembling, vines twitching. "We preserve what is left. It will suffice. We do not take from others!"

"Pah." Jazriel spat directly on Wyliff's knobby foot. "That's what I think of you, Tree Man. You cannot oppose us, you and the little ones like the stupid old hob here. Your power has dwindled more than ours. Now, leave!" Jazriel's eyes narrowed when Wyliff made no move. "So, you need a demonstration. Will this prove you are outmatched?" He extended his hands toward Wyliff, palms out, fingers spread apart and tensed. Closing his eyes, Jazriel's face went blank. The glow surrounding him flared, and from each fingertip a flame grew. "Wood burns so easily," he said conversationally.

Exerting every ounce of will, Ben strained until suddenly he was able to move. He ran forward, head down, catching Jazriel in the stomach, making him stagger back. The flames winked out instantly. Ben desperately tried to reach Yvonne, but he felt himself plucked from behind and dangled like a kitten. Wyliff's voice boomed over his head. "Nothing is certain, Jazriel. As you see."

Wyliff strode back into the forest carrying Ben, Billy Blind trotting at his side. Ben struggled briefly, but realized it was futile. He twisted his neck so he could see what Jazriel and the Fey were doing. They were just as Wyliff had left them. Jazriel stared after Wyliff, a look on his face — it almost looked like fear. Then, rage twisted his features and a simple hand gesture started up the music again. Jazriel mounted his bike, and he and his henchmen revved their engines and began circling the heath.

"Put me down!"

It seemed that Ben had been yelling this over and over, but the Green Man kept marching away. Billy Blind chortled and poked at Ben every time he spoke, his fear of Jazriel gone now that they were no longer near the Fey host.

"Don't like being treated like a babby, do you, bor?" The hob's eyes keenly scanned Ben's face. "But don't you forget, that's just what you are in our world — a babby who knows nothing, a babby who could have got himself blasted back there. Don't you know just what Jazriel could have done to you?"

Before Ben could frame a reply, Wyliff's fingers released their grip and he fell. Dusting himself off, he turned furiously, to yell his rage at Wyliff and Billy Blind, but stopped himself. Wyliff was standing still —

no tremors, no rustling of leaves. Clear amber fluid, like sap, streamed from his eyes, causing the leaves of his beard to glisten in the moonlight. His mouth was open in a small keening cry. Straining his ears, Ben could make out words that repeated over and over. "Maybe too late, too late. Maybe too strong, too strong."

"Ah, bollocks, he's going into one of his trances again!" Billy Blind was standing, hands on hips, his rough features screwed up in distaste. "I can't be doing with all this. Bloody Jazriel knew what he was doing, all right. Show a Green Man fire and that's it — too close to being a tree's the problem."

Despite his fear and confusion, Ben couldn't help smiling at the hob's irreverence. He was suddenly conscious of how hard his heart was beating and the dryness of his mouth that made it hard to speak, even though questions were burning inside him. Swallowing hard and running his tongue around his mouth finally freed his voice. "What the fuck's happening, Billy Blind?" Even as he spoke, he felt like laughing; the question sounded so banal and had little chance of being answered.

"Old Leaf-face isn't much of a one for explanations, is he, bor, so it's all left up to the Billy Blind, isn't it? Be patient, and you'll get your answers. But don't rush me, we hobs do hate to be rushed!" Billy Blind looked up at Ben and then busied himself with one of his many pouches, pulling out small leaf-wrapped packages, which he placed on the ground. He flopped down heavily, resting his back against one of Wyliff's legs as if he were a convenient tree trunk. Seeing Ben's shock, he laughed. "Oh, don't worry about him. He can't feel it. Might as well make some use of him, until he gets himself collected up and out of his bejabbers. Could be an hour or two, if I know anything about it. So why don't you make yourself comfortable, mebbe have a little something to eat to pass the time?"

Ben glanced at his watch. It was not yet midnight. How could that be? It seemed like hours since he had crept out of the cottage.

"Got somewhere to go, have you?" Billy Blind's laughter was raucous. "Know your way home?"

Ben realized he had no idea where they were — just some piece of woodland somewhere around Norwich. He spread his hands helplessly, trying not to be annoyed by the amusement he saw in the hob's eye, and sat down.

Raising his voice over Wyliff's persistent drone, Billy Blind asked, "So what's he told you, and what have you worked out?"

Words poured out — words that had been locked up inside Ben since all the weirdness had started. He wasn't sure that there was any order or logic to the way it spewed out — the fight with Baz, Yvonne's collapse, the way Wyliff had stalked him, his cryptic pronouncements.

And now it had all come together in what they had just seen — Yvonne somehow in thrall to Jazriel, and Baz ... Ben wasn't sure what was happening with Baz.

Then Ben stared at Billy Blind, waiting for a response.

"Do you fancy a bit?" the hob asked, holding out what looked like a shriveled ear. Seeing the look on Ben's face, he added, "It's just a mushroom, tha's all. It's not Fey food. You needn't worry about that. Eating it isn't going to bind you to me forever. In fact, it's from your garden!" When Ben still hesitated, he popped it into his own mouth, chewing noisily. "Ah, lubbly grub!"

Billy Blind jerked his head back toward Wyliff. "He's led you a right old dance, hasn't he? Funny old feller, don't see that much of him, normally. Tends to keep to himself. Spends most of his time standing around with trees. What a life, eh?" The hob chortled to himself, but stopped when he saw that Ben was not laughing. "Get to the point, Billy Blind!" he admonished himself. "It's all down to them Fey, especially that blasted Jazriel." He shook his head. "Never have liked that one, always got to be wary around him even when he was just a boy. Don't ever let him and his cronies catch you alone." Billy Blind shuddered.

Ben's impatience got the better of him. "Who is he, this Jazriel? Why is he taking humans?"

"Now that's the nub of it." Billy Blind rubbed his nose reflectively. "That's what we'd all like to know. He's using 'em somehow, and it's upset the balance of things.

And it's going to get worse."

Ben sighed. Perhaps the hob did know something of what was going on, but getting it out of him was painful.

Billy Blind seemed to sense Ben's impatience. "It's hard, bor. It's hard to explain. You humans don't have the knowledge anymore. You don't even believe in us." The hob's eyes glinted with what looked suspiciously like tears. "The Fey, the seelie host, they were always the powerful ones, with their king and all. Us littl'uns lived in their shadow, and if things were good for them, then they were good for us, too. Them as like Wyliff, the big'uns, they live by their own selves, owing nothing to no one. But now, now it's you humans who are the powerful ones. You take over the wild spaces and build, pushing us out. Havriel, tha's Jazriel's father, he just accepted that that was the way things were now, that there would always be a place, if it be only a little space, where we would be safe, as long as we stayed away from you lot."

Ben burst out, "He was the bound one, right?" The hob's words were shifting things in his mind.

Billy Blind hung his head. "Aye, that was him. Jazriel has cast him down, unnatural though it be. Jazriel has turned the court. Like old Leaf-face said, 'Seelie becomes unseelie'!"

"Unseelie is the dark way?" Ben didn't wait for Billy Blind to confirm this. "Somehow, this Jazriel is planning to use humans, to live in our world. That's why he's got Yvonne." He jumped to his feet, pacing. "But why her? And why does Wyliff think I can stop this? All he gave me was some crap about anger and the old blood."

Ben was shocked when Billy Blind laughed long and hard. "Blood and lights! How can you humans be so ignorant? How can you forget so quickly? The old blood, the blood of the heroes, the blood of them as has had the sight. I see it, bor, it burns through you like quicksilver. Your father has it, too, the blood of the smith." Billy Blind giggled, looked slyly up at Ben. "I bin watching. Mind you, your da's hard to miss. Talk about loud! Have to be careful, too, because he has knowledge of us still, only he doesn't dare let himself see." The hob sighed. "Blood of the smith — Wayland we called him. He had other names in other places. It's what makes you strong, makes you different. Makes you hard to be around." Shuddering but smiling, Billy Blind asked, "I'm right there, aren't I?"

"I don't know." Ben's head ached with it all. "But Yvonne — why her? Wyliff said she had the old blood, too, but we're not related. I just met her a few days ago."

"Her!" Billy Blind crowed. "Her! She's always had the sight, strong, saw us all from when she was just a sad little mawther, creeping around the woods, crying often as not. We tried to stay out of her way." He spat, as if to get rid of a lingering foul taste in his mouth. "Especially after they made a pet of her: Jazriel and his bully boys, Fitch and Quoil. It was them as was riding with him tonight."

Fitch and Quoil. That's why the name Jazriel had seemed so familiar to Ben. These were the names Mrs. Lea had said, the names of Yvonne's imaginary playmates. He shuddered, wondering what they had done with her then. And what did they have planned for her now? "But," he protested, "how can she be here? I saw her in the hospital."

"Hostibal, now what's that then? Don't know no such creature as hostibal." The hob didn't wait for an answer. "When the Fey take you, they leave something in your place, sometimes a changeling — that's one of their own kind if you're a babby — or a stock if'n you're a grown one. Stocks aren't really alive; they are just enough to fool most."

"We leave!" The voice came from above. Wyliff's eyes still flared with panic, but at least he seemed aware of both them and his surroundings. He stretched out a hand toward Ben, but Ben sidestepped the grasping fingers, determined not to be forced into anything.

"Hold you hard, Leaf-face!" Billy Blind planted himself in front of Wyliff, a quiver of outrage seeming to increase his bulk. "Me and the boy have been talking while you went off into your little panic, and we want some bloody answers!"

Wyliff shivered. Ben forced down the anger, tried to keep his voice calm. "You said that I had to see. Well, I've seen. It's starting to make sense. This Jazriel has Yvonne. Why, Billy Blind doesn't know, and neither do I. Do you?" The last words blasted out accusingly.

Wyliff closed his eyes. He breathed deeply. "They seek to finish what they started when she was a child, but now she resists them. She knows the cost — to her, to us, to this." Wyliff's arms flailed wildly, as if he wanted to encompass the whole world. From beneath his closed eyelids, traced with fine green veins, more amber tears flowed. His voice when he finally spoke was a whisper. "I cannot go against them. I thought I could. I thought that the old contract between Fey and the Green World would hold. Jazriel does not abide by that which is old. I will burn. He will burn me."

Ben felt something clench inside. Wyliff's size, his strength, seemed diminished. Ben looked at Billy Blind, but the hob was staring openmouthed at Wyliff, his eyes wet and shiny.

"Screw that! What about Yvonne!" Ben was aware that he was shouting, that Billy Blind had put both hands over his ears. "If you can't do it, who can? Someone, something must be able to oppose a Fey?"

Wyliff's eyes opened. "You," he said simply. "You can

get her back."

"Ah, come off it." Ben's protest was involuntary, but he knew, deep down, that the Green Man was right. It wasn't just that Wyliff had marked him, chosen him. Yvonne had sought him out. She saw something in him, something that promised help to her.

Billy Blind snorted — a look from Wyliff kept him quiet, but did nothing to erase his look of contempt.

"We leave." Wyliff reached out his hands, taking both Ben's and Billy Blind's. "Tomorrow night we plan. Now we leave."

Billy Blind's outraged "We, what's this we?" tailed off as Ben felt himself stretched once again. This time, he kept his balance, arriving by the willow in the back garden of the cottage. He looked around for Wyliff, but he was not there. Billy Blind was trotting off at high speed toward the brick archway that linked their cottage to its neighbor. The hob waved an impatient hand when Ben called his name, but did not turn or stop. When he reached the archway, he seemed to insinuate himself into a crack in the wall.

Ben looked around. The full moon still hung heavily in the sky, silvering the plants that surrounded him. The peaceful, beautiful scene did not move him — it was charged with danger and menace. Shivering, he made for the cottage.

The back door creaked a little as he opened it, freezing him in his tracks, but Lars' snoring racketed down the stairs to greet him.

Oh, Lars, he thought, if only you knew!

Even in the cottage, Ben felt cold. He crept up the stairs, undressed hurriedly and threw himself onto his bed, pulling the duvet up to his chin, waiting for its warmth to soothe him. Sleep did not come. As he reached across to switch on his bedside lamp, Ben glanced at his clock radio. The display read 12:01 AM.

Sunday

Thin, early evening sunshine made the pastel-painted beach huts glow. Ben stared moodily at them. Where the hell was Lars? He had promised he would only be twenty minutes, and he must have been gone for at least an hour.

"Just one more church," Lars had wheedled. "You'll find it interesting, I promise. There's this really neat little statue they call Southwold Jack."

"No!" Ben had shouted. "I've had it up to here with churches today, especially the ones that turn out to be locked up after we spend ages trying to find them." He grimaced at the memory. A day of waiting until it was dark so he could find Wyliff and Billy Blind again had not been appealing, nor had a day of worrying about Yvonne and what Jazriel had planned for her. In bed the previous night, Ben had dreamed up mad schemes: he'd go to the hospital again and somehow convince them that what was in the bed was not Yvonne but some weird supernatural doppelgänger, and that they needed to get the police searching the woods around Norwich. Yeah, right. Like anyone would listen. He'd probably get himself locked up. Lars would know what he was talking about, but he wouldn't believe him. Baz had preyed on his mind, too. Had he been taken the same way as Yvonne? Was there a stock, a mock Baz worrying and fooling his family? Or was Baz different? Jazriel had said he'd come willingly. What did that mean?

By the time morning came, Ben had felt exhausted, desperate for a way not to think, so when Lars had suggested they take a drive down through Suffolk to the sea, he had accepted readily — which had obviously surprised Lars. But Ben was now regretting his decision as a thin wind chilled him to the bone. "Are you sure you don't have anything else you want to do?" Lars had asked. Then he'd laughed. "Forget I said that. This is great. We'll have fun. Boy bonding time." With the last words, Lars had put a finger in his mouth and pretended to vomit. "There's a couple of churches we might stop at on the way — interesting carvings — but that shouldn't take too long. One of the guys at the university told me about some good restaurants. We'll eat out — lunch and an early dinner — get back in time for you to do that homework. *A Midsummer Night's Dream*, wasn't it?"

Was it? Then Ben had remembered that he'd given the play as an excuse for rooting around in Lars' books. "Uh, no, it's all done." Lars looked skeptical, but he had not pressed, obviously determined not to jeopardize the trip to which Ben had so surprisingly agreed.

Lars' couple of churches had turned out to be many. Ben truly had lost count. They all seemed to be in tiny villages hidden along winding, narrow, leaf-tunneled roads. Many churches were no longer in regular use, which meant hunting for the key holders. If they were found, then Lars' enthusiasm usually gained them entrance, if not a guided tour. Ben had not had to work hard to play the role of the surly, bored teenager. Twice, though, he had nearly let his guard down.

Ben had prevented any attempts at conversation on the drive from Norwich by jamming on his earphones as soon as he got into the car and cranking the volume. Despite this, Ben had fallen into a deep sleep that left him blurry and disoriented when Lars brought the car to a halt.

Lifting one earphone gently, Lars had said something — something that Ben didn't catch apart from "Green Man."

Before he could stop himself, Ben had asked, "Wyliff? Where?"

"Wyliff? Who's Wyliff?" Panic flared in Ben, hearing Lars say Wyliff's name. Lars had waited for a reply, his eyes not leaving Ben's face. Then Ben had almost seen the decision being made not to press him farther, a decision that, by the worry creasing Lars' forehead, had not come easily. When Lars had finally spoken, his attempt to sound normal rang false. "No, that's not the name of the village, though it's weird enough." Lars had shaken his shaggy head. "We're in Little Whelnetham. Wait here. I'll find someone to let us in."

Ben had sat in a cold sweat, reliving his close call. The sweat had increased when he found himself staring up at the church roof under the tower and meeting the pained gaze of a wooden carving. All it needed were the amber tears and it would have reproduced the anguish on Wyliff's face as he had keened his misery. Ben didn't want to look at the carving, but couldn't help it. Lars had barely glanced at it. Instead, he had watched Ben.

In the car afterward and through lunch, Lars had talked nonstop, but Ben felt that he was working at it, while his mind was puzzling something else entirely. He had talked about the various types of Green Man carvings, and he offered theories to explain them: they represented a spirit of the woods, or a general nature spirit, or were racial memories of forest-dwelling tribes, the original inhabitants of England. Ben had done his best to keep his face expressionless and not to react at all, but it was hard. He burned with the knowledge of what Wyliff was, of how close Lars was to that truth.

The other nasty moment had come at the last church Ben had gone into, Holy Trinity in Blythburgh. A vast building rising like a ship out of the flat land, it was bound on one side by an estuary. The church had seemed cold and menacing, and for the first time they were not alone — about fifteen visitors dotted the huge interior, gazing up at the high ceiling. Ben had looked up warily, but no Green Men stared back at him, just brightly painted medieval angels with bland faces. In typical fashion, Lars had started talking to an old man sitting in one of the pews. His thick accent had made him hard to understand, but with a bit of prompting from Lars, he had launched into a history of the church. If Ben had been in a better mood, he might have taken a certain relish in the angels — their bullet wounds dated back, according to local legend, to the Puritans, who had tried to shoot them down from their celestial perch. Instead, he had spent the time wondering what Wyliff had meant about "making plans."

"And the black dogs." The words had eased themselves into the conversation, and suddenly Ben had listened attentively as the old man recounted the tale of a fateful Sunday in August 1577, when a black dog, "a hound of hell," had rampaged through two churches in Suffolk. In Bungay, it had killed two parishioners in front of the altar, and here, in Blythburgh, the fury of its passage had brought down the spire, killing and maiming the congregation. "People say you still see them dogs around here, stalking the laneways at night. Never means anything but bad." The man had shaken his head theatrically, but his words had sent shivers down Ben's spine as he remembered the two dogs he had seen with Jazriel. He had suddenly needed to be outside, in sunshine with the wind fresh on his face.

"Lars, let's go," he had said, and there must have been something in his voice, because Lars made hurried apologies to the old man, who was suggesting that he might remember some more stories if they repaired to the White Hart pub just down the road.

Lars had looked quizzically at Ben when they got back to the car, but had accepted his excuse of feeling a little light-headed. "Maybe it's getting close to dinner," Lars had said. "We'll eat at The Crown in Southwold. Ten minutes away, no more."

But now, Ben was standing on a beach, waiting. The Crown didn't serve food until 7:00 PM, and Lars had set his heart on eating there. That was when he had suggested just one more church.

Ben looked down the beach, more pebbles than sand. There were few people on it: couples walking, some with dogs; a family with small children in brightly colored sweaters skimming stones out on the waves. He had walked its length twice. On the long pier, he had found half an hour of amusement, but now Ben was bored, and as the clouds drifted over the sun, he was cold, too. What the hell, he thought, I'll go back to the pub and wait for Lars there.

Ben started up the beach, his sneakers sinking into the stones. "Aaagh!" A sharp pain seared through his toes. Moving his foot gingerly back, Ben crouched down to see what he had hit. There was nothing large there, not the old concrete or driftwood he was expecting. Instead, in a declivity that seemed almost deliberate, two stones lay, like speckled eggs cradled in a nest. Ben picked them up, turning them over in his fingers. Although they were of different colors — one whitish with gray flecks, and the other a dark tan — each stone had a hole running through it, so perfect that they could have been drilled. The stones felt warm, as if demanding that he finger them.

"What you got there?" Lars was kneeling beside him, his hand extended.

"Just stones." Ben made to put them in his pocket, but Lars gestured impatiently and Ben was forced to hand them over.

Lars sucked his teeth and then whistled quietly. "So that's how you've been spending your time, eh? Two of them! Must have taken you a while!" He grinned at Ben from under the heavy swath of hair that fell over his forehead. "Yeah, yeah, I know. I was gone far too long. I'm sorry, but —"

Ben interrupted. "Why do you think it took me a long time to find these? What the hell are they?" He knew his tone was abrupt, but he also knew that the stones were important somehow, that he had been meant to find them. "Give them back, okay?"

Lars handed over the stones, his face puzzled. "Sure, of course. Cool it. They're called hag stones around here, Ben. Folklorists call them 'self-bored stones.' Traditionally, they either protect a person or animal from a fairy or witch's magic, or enable a person to see fairies and other supernatural creatures." He laughed. "But all that's from before people knew the effect of wave action on rocks. You're some kind of lucky, though, Benny-boy. People can spend their whole lives looking and never find a single one!" He stretched, joints cracking, then chuckled. "Maybe you have the sight, like your grandfather."

For a moment, Ben was puzzled as to how anyone could ever think of anything mystical in association with his practical, down-to-earth grandfather in Toronto. Then it dawned on him — Lars was talking about his own father. All Ben knew was that Lars' father had left Canada some years back for Iceland, the country where his own parents had come from. Is this what Wyliff and Billy Blind meant about the old blood? Was this something that ran in his family? Ben winced, but didn't speak, hoping that Lars would drop the subject.

"Must be it," Lars steamrollered on. "You must take after my old man, your afi. He was always claiming to see things, to know things before they happened. Hell, that's why he took off — told my mother that he had to find his roots, that something was calling him." Lars' laugh was bitter. "Or, maybe none of the men in this family are big on commitment and responsibility — as I'm sure your mother drummed into you." Lars spoke again, quickly, before Ben could respond. "Ignore that last remark, Ben. Cheap shot. But things did happen around my dad, still do — I visited him a couple of years ago — and things are happening around you, too."

Ben winced, but remained silent. He tried a diversion, making his voice as snotty and dismissive as he could. "I didn't look for the stones, Lars. I was just walking up the beach to go back to The Crown — tired of freezing my ass off waiting for you — and my foot stubbed against them. They found me." Ben enjoyed the look of surprise on his father's face. "C'mon, let's go eat. I'm starving. That restaurant's got to be open by now."

The Crown was open, and Ben and Lars eventually settled themselves at a mismatched wooden table for two after a minor to-do as Lars tried to seat them at the end of a long table, obviously eager to strike up conversations with whoever might join them as the bar filled up. When he shambled off to the bar to place their drink orders and get menu sheets, Ben looked idly around. He mentally calculated how long it would take them to eat and drive back to Norwich — maybe three hours in all. Damn, he thought. By the time he waited for Lars to go to bed, it might be past midnight before he could sneak out. It was not that he would miss anything; it was much more — a feeling of commitment, that this was something he could do, that he needed to do before things got out of hand. He feared for Yvonne — if she could not hold out much longer, what would happen?

"A bit fancy, but it looks tasty!" Lars was pushing a sheet of paper in front of Ben's face. "I like the sound of the wild boar sausage with a caramelized onion tarte. Very Viking if you ignore the tarte bit!" He immediately took a swig of dark beer, leaving a creamy froth on his mustache. He pushed a smaller mug across to Ben. "It's a half of shandy — beer mixed with ginger beer. The barman said that lemonade would make it too sweet." Seeing Ben's involuntary shudder at the thought of beer mixed with lemons, Lars laughed. "Nah, Ben, lemonade is different here. Trust me." When Ben still seemed reluctant, Lars took his hands and folded them around the mug. "Go on, live a little. Don't tell me you've never had beer before."

Rather than argue, Ben took a sip. The sourness of the beer was a shock, nothing like the cool beers he was used to back home, sneaking them at his friends' houses, but it was softened by the spicy sweetness of the ginger beer. Conscious of Lars' eyes intent on his face, he nodded. "It's okay."

"Good, good!" Lars' response was overly hearty, making Ben wonder why. Lars caught the attention of one of the passing waitresses, only to be told that he had to place the order at the bar. He looked questioningly at Ben.

"Same as you," Ben blurted, not wanting to waste any more time.

The silence as they waited for their food was oppressive. Ben stared around the room or looked at the table. Every time he glanced in Lars' direction, he'd catch him looking at him, although he tried to pretend he wasn't. The fourth time it happened, Lars started to laugh.

"This is bloody ridiculous. I treat you like a time bomb. KAAAABOOOM!" His loud imitation of an explosion, complete with appropriate hand gestures and spit spray, caused heads to turn. Instead of going red, as Ben would have done, Lars half rose from his seat and bowed, smiling hugely. Shocked diners busied themselves with their food or resumed suddenly urgent conversations.

"Do I embarrass you, Ben?" Lars' voice was quiet. "Is it really painful to spend time with me? Is it merely dislike, or is it full-blown hatred?" He stretched his hands out in front of him, looked down at their suntanned backs, before staring hard at Ben. "I don't know. Sometimes, I think it's all of the above. What a success!" He tried to laugh, but gave up.

Shit. Ben didn't want to deal with this now. He looked frantically around.

"No, Ben, there's nowhere to go. You can't stomp off to your room or to the woods. And what is it with those woods? One more subject that we can't talk about, apparently. You could rush out into the street, but you still have to get home, and we still have to coexist. We can eat our food in silence, drive home in silence, but I'll still have those questions, still feel I'm failing at this father stuff. Ah, shit, Ben!" Lars closed his eyes. His smile, when he opened them again, was wry. "What's really important is the fact that you're so goddamn unhappy. I don't want to add to it, but I do want to help. Tell me what I should do."

Ben was saved from having to answer by the cheerful bustling waitress, who plonked down their food, nearly dropping one of the napkined rolls of cutlery.

"So, it's going to be silence, eh?" Lars methodically unwrapped his knife and fork, placing them tidily on either side of his plate, but he made no attempt to eat.

"It's not that simple." Ben spoke almost without intention. "It's not just you. It's …" He struggled to find the words to describe the complex mess inside his head. "I don't want to be here — and I don't mean England," he said, as Lars tried to interrupt. "I want …" He thought hard, trying to describe the ache of longing inside him always lurking behind his thoughts. "I want everything to be the way it was ... before." As the words came out, he realized that it really was that simple: all it would take to make him happy was to have back his old life, an imperfect life, for sure — he and his mother had fought often enough — but a life that had certainty.

Lars sighed. "If I could, Ben, I'd make it so. I can't. I can't bring your mother back. I couldn't even have prevented her dying. No one could. She didn't see a doctor until it was way too late."

Anger flooded Ben. "Right. So it's all her fault!" He pushed his plate away, untouched, and moved to the edge of his chair, poised for flight.

"No, goddamn it! Calm down, Ben!" Lars reached across and grabbed Ben's hand, ignoring his attempts to twist it free. "Cancer is random. All I'm saying is that if she had gone earlier, we would all have had more time — time to get to know each other, to work things out — and wouldn't have had to deal with it all in a rush. But that didn't happen, and wishing won't make it happen. It's not my fault, and it's certainly not yours. We've got to find a way through all this." Lars let go of Ben's hand. "Ah, shit. Things would have been a damn sight easier if I hadn't been built up to be the big, bad bogeyman."

Ben sent his chair crashing to the floor. Ignoring the shocked stares, he hissed at Lars. "Don't you fucking dare criticize Mom! Eat your dinner. I'll wait in the car." He walked as quickly as he could, pushing past the waitress who had started over to see what was wrong. He could hear Lars' voice rumbling in the background, and then the lights of the car flashed once as Lars used the remote to unlock it. Ben threw himself into the front seat, turning his face to the side window so that he didn't have to look at Lars or acknowledge his rueful "Well, I guess that's one restaurant we won't be eating at again."

Lars pleaded that they needed to talk, that he was sorry if he'd offended Ben.

"Stick your apology!" Ben said to the window, his breath fogging the glass. He grabbed his Walkman and played the loudest CD he could find, keeping his eyes on the buildings, then the trees that flashed past, aware of the tense misery that came from Lars in waves.

It was hypnotic — until the car suddenly swerved. Ben's forehead banged hard against the glass, and he turned ready to let rip with a mouthful of abuse about Lars' driving, but Lars was hunched over the wheel, his knuckles white, his face beaded with sweat, struggling to control the car as they approached the turnoff for Cringleford. Ben took his headphones off. A rushing noise filled his ears, and it was several seconds before Ben realized that it was the sound of the wind, a wind so powerful that it was buffeting the small car. Trees were swaying wildly, and Ben saw power lines come crackling down, sending blue sparks arcing into the night sky. Then the lights went out — streetlights, houses, everything.

"Lars! What's happening?"

His face taut with effort, Lars ground out a reply, saving all his energy and concentration for driving. "Since Beccles. Some kind of freak storm."

It was eerie, traveling in total darkness, and Ben was glad when they turned down Church Farm Lane. The narrow road had a dense hedge on one side that would give some protection from the wild winds, and the trees on the other side had been carefully planted some distance apart.

"Shit!" Lars had been traveling slowly, but even so, when he slammed on the brakes, the small car skidded and slewed to one side before coming to a shuddering halt in front of a tree that had fallen across the entrance to the cottages.

"Are you okay?" Lars peered anxiously at Ben, and Ben saw that Lars' hands were shaking slightly. "Let's get out and see if we can move it."

Ben felt tired and slightly sick. "Look!" He pointed past the tree to flashlights bobbing amongst a knot of people, ordinary-looking people, not the black-garbed trio he had been dreading.

A voice hailed them out of the darkness. "Are you chaps all right?" Ben had seen the speaker on week-ends, a tall, elegant man whose jeans were always immaculately clean and pressed. "Bloody wind brought the tree down.

Just minutes ago! Terrible noise, shook the cottages, rattled windows. I think we can shift it if we work together. Otherwise, you'll have to leave your car there, but you should be able to clamber through." The man was used to giving orders, Ben thought, and he waited to see whether Lars' dislike of being told what to do would surface, but Lars just nodded agreement and took up a position midway down the tree trunk, then signaled for Ben to join him. The tree was only a few years old, and it was easy to lift it and then lay it alongside the road.

All Ben wanted was to get inside and wait until he could find Wyliff and Billy Blind, but the neighbors seemed unusually sociable. There were introductions and much talk about the storm.

"Haven't seen anything like this since 1987," one of the men said. "We had dustbins flying past bedroom windows then. Let's hope this isn't that bad." As he spoke, there was a huge rumbling crash and a tearing sound from the cottages. Ben sprinted through the archway and into the back garden. When the others arrived, he was standing by the willow, which had been torn up by the roots and lay corpselike across the lawn, its crown pointing to the woods.

The winds suddenly ceased.

"Bloody hell!" a voice cried. "Think of the damage if it had fallen the other way. The cottage would have been smashed."

Inside his head, Ben wailed, "Wyliff! Oh, Wyliff!"

"Billy Blind," he called quietly. "Wyliff?"

There was no answer.

Turning his back on the garden, Ben touched the wall where he had seen the hob disappear last night. All he felt beneath his fingers was brick — solid brick, except for a tiny crack.

He had expected Billy Blind, if not Wyliff as well, to be waiting. Where the hell were they? Had they taken off without him? Bastards! He kicked a stone from his path. Just set him up, involve him in weird shit, then dump him.

It had taken forever for the neighbors to disperse; one had produced a bottle of whisky for everyone. "Good for shock!" had been his laconic comment. Ben hadn't wanted to stay, but he had no choice, and it soon became evident that nearly everyone felt uneasy, although they articulated it in ways that fit the mundane, normal tenor of their lives. "The weather's all shot to pot," one had said. "Bloody global warming. No normal lately, is there? Almost makes you feel like you're at the mercy of forces you don't understand." Ben had shuddered.

Lars had been quiet, smiling wryly when their immediate neighbor, whom they'd seen a little more of than the others, said, "Isn't that up your alley, Tryggvason, all this spooky old stuff?"

"Yeah," Lars had said. "Bad weather, crop failure, sudden illnesses — those would have been seen as the work of some supernatural being or force, maybe fairies." When this had prompted a guffaw of disbelieving laughter, he had added, "Not those pretty little winged things in gauzy dresses. That was the Victorians' attempt to make them safe. Fairies in the old beliefs were wild, dangerous, amoral creatures. They —" Lars' eyes had gleamed and his voice had become animated, but then he had looked over at Ben and stopped mid-sentence. "Look, thanks for the drink and helping us get home. But it's been a long day, so I think we'll head in. I'll call in a tree surgeon tomorrow to deal with the willow, and he can get rid of the other one at the same time. Okay?"

Inside, Lars just said, "I am truly tired, Ben. There's no electricity and I haven't got any candles, so I'm going to bed. Do what you like — just don't burn the place down lighting matches."

So Ben had waited in the dark, peering out until he saw the last person leave, their flashlight beam bobbing to their cottage.

He returned to the garden, grateful for the moonlight and that the wild wind had not returned. The air had a curiously flat feel to it. He strained his ears, listening for any sound or movement, but it was unnaturally still.

The clearing. He would try the clearing. Perhaps that was where they were waiting for him — in Wyliff's vague way, nothing had been said as to where they should meet. Ben thought briefly about getting a flashlight, but decided against it. He knew the way well enough, had even walked it in the dark. A flashlight might draw unwanted attention, and the last thing he needed was some busybody neighbor calling the police to report a prowler in the woods.

Ben set off, slowly so as not to trip in the near dark. He shivered, trying to rid himself of the strange sensation that if he had fur, it would be standing up in a ridge down his back. His mouth was dry and he could hear the beat of his pulse in his ears. About fifty paces into the trees, Ben realized why he felt so uneasy — the silence was total. He was the only moving thing, but he knew that in burrows and nests, creatures were hunkered down, watching. Was that where Billy Blind was, too? Was the hob sitting it out safely in whatever he called home?

The clearing was just ahead. Ben quickened his pace until he was going at a fast trot. "Wyliff?" Strangely distorted, his voice echoed into the trees. Ben froze at the edge of the clearing.

A rustle on the far side of the clearing, a small rustle — someone or something was moving in the trees.

Ben strained, trying to see, but it was too dark. The noise came again, this time closer, just to his left. Then it was to his right. Then behind him. Now he could see low bushes moving around the clearing. Were Wyliff and the hob playing games? Impossible. Then fear replaced puzzlement.

"Ben." His name. "Ben." Someone was saying his name, drawing out the single syllable as if this was just the sound that breath made. He turned slowly round, trying to work out the direction of the sound. As he did so, other voices joined in, with the same breathy delivery. A figure emerged from the shadows, walking with a strange jerking gait into the center of the clearing.

Baz.

His face was very white in the moonlight, with an unhealthy sheen of sweat. Circles like bruises under his eyes made him look older and somehow diminished, wizened. He smiled at Ben, a smile that slipped and wavered. "All right, mate?" he said, and the eerie quality of the voice that delivered the familiar, banal words chilled Ben.

Ben said nothing, calculating whether he could outrun Baz. He started to edge backward slowly, but stopped when more figures joined Baz — cronies from the day of the fight. They remained silent, on either side of Baz.

"Who's been a naughty boy, then? Causing trouble, or is it that you're going to cause trouble?" Baz nodded his head, reminding Ben of bobble-headed dogs in tacky souvenir shops. The nodding seemed involuntary, as if, once started, Baz couldn't stop it. "Yeah, that's it, isn't it, boys?" His head still jerking, he looked sideways at each of his two companions, but they kept their impassive gazes on Ben. "Oh, yes, they've had your card marked right from the start, only they couldn't do nothing about it, see? Not without more power, and that's what they're getting now." With a great effort, the strain showing on his face, Baz finally stopped nodding and took a step toward Ben. "We're all getting what we want now. Look!" he said, and he pointed to a bush, changing the gesture to a beckoning one.

Ben watched in horror as a rabbit came from beneath the bush, slithering on its belly. The unnaturalness of its movement was emphasized by the way its limbs spasmed, the muscles seeming at war with one another. Its eyes rolled and a fine line of blood furrowed down from one quivering nostril. Finally, it stopped, panting close to Baz's foot. He kicked at it, but his leg seemed loose and he missed.

"Way cool!" Baz said, staring down at the rabbit, licking his lips. "Start with little things, Jazriel says, then move on to bigger ones." He looked slyly at Ben. "People. That'll be the best."

Ben felt sick to his stomach, but his mind raced, making connections, and the thoughts that formed

BARRINGTON PUBLIC LIBRARY
BARRINGTON, R.I.

scared him even more. This is what Jazriel had done to Baz, what he and his friends were becoming. Surely they weren't so stupid that they couldn't see the terrible price for such a pathetic morsel of magic?

"Look at you," he found himself saying. "Look at the state you're in. How can you let this happen? That bastard Jazriel is using you. Can't you see that?"

"Nah," Baz said. "It's not like that. You just don't get it. Things are changing. We're helping to change them." His face twisted, the features seeming to slip loosely over the bone beneath. "It'd be faster if she'd help." His voice was dying away to a mumble that Ben had to strain to hear. "Don't see what's so special about her, why Jazriel makes so much of her — not when she won't speak, won't bloody do anything!"

"Yvonne, that's who you mean. What do you know about her? Where is she? Why are they keeping her?" As the questions poured out, Ben forgot his fear and moved forward, ready to shake the answers from Baz.

Without a word, Baz's friends interposed their bodies between Baz and Ben. One shoved Ben hard, sending him staggering backward. Although there was a surprising strength behind the blow, the hand felt flaccid and cold.

Safe behind the barrier of flesh and bone, Baz laughed. "Stupid bitch, that's what she is, a stupid bitch!" He spat the words out. "She could have anything. They'd give her anything." The words trailed off and Baz peered over his bodyguards' shoulders at Ben. "She's like you. She has the old blood, the strong blood, the blood that will forge a new race!" Baz sniggered. "Only the old blood has its own power, see. She can resist a little, like you did. Jazriel didn't like that, not one bit. She doesn't have to do what they want. She has to be willing, and nothing Jazriel can do can alter that, can it, boys?" Baz put a hand on each of his friends' shoulders and then vaulted over their heads, landing heavily in front of Ben.

A shiver went down Ben's spine.

"We haven't come here to talk," Baz said. "We've been sent. We're to finish what I started, get you out of the way, boy." The manic giggle came again. "Just like Jazriel and his boys are doing to the tree man and the little feller."

Ben couldn't move, just stared as the shock of the words sank in. It was only when Baz shambled forward, his hands outstretched and twitching, that fear galvanized Ben into flight — back through the trees, branches tearing at his clothes and face. Ben could hear the others behind him, knew they were near, but he was faster. Baz had wasted time, had enjoyed taunting him too much, and that might just let Ben escape.

Ben burst out of the trees into the garden of the cottage. Lights blazed from the kitchen, but the upstairs was in darkness — the power had come back on. Baz and his friends were gaining on him. He heard the thud of their feet. Careering around the corpse of the willow, Ben threw himself at the back door, launching himself into the kitchen. He jammed home the bolts at the door's top and bottom and leaned his back against it, sliding down until he was sitting on the cold flagstones, his head on his knees as he fought for breath.

He felt rather than heard the soft tapping on the door, a reverberation that beat against his spine. Baz's face was pressed against the window, his features squashed and distorted, his tongue hanging out in an awful parody of a dog. As Ben stared in horror, Baz's hand came up and he gestured as he had done to the rabbit. It was like a tug inside Ben's head, but a tiny one. Ben reared to his feet, reaching for the light switch. With one downward sweep, he brought darkness to the room, and he raced up the stairs. In his bedroom, he dragged the curtains roughly across the window. Only when he was satisfied that he could not see out, nor could anyone see in, did he flop onto the bed. It was a long time before his heart slowed down. A wild melee of images and feelings pulsed to its manic beat — Jazriel and his cronies chasing Wyliff and Billy Blind, the Green Man and the hob ducking and diving from flames; Yvonne's tightly clenched face as she resisted the Fey, a prisoner on her glass throne and the center of Jazriel's grandly evil plan; Baz crouching outside, waiting; and the rabbit lying helpless and panting on the grass.

Monday

"Ben! Ben! Wake up!"

Forcing his eyes open, Ben found Lars looking down on him, the hand that had shaken him awake still on his shoulder. He couldn't believe that he had slept.

"My god, look at the state of you!" Lars' innocent words made him shudder, as they mimicked his own words to Baz. "You slept in your clothes?"

Ben sat up, ran his hands through his hair. He felt as if someone had fried his brain. Why couldn't Lars leave him alone? What was his problem?

"We've both overslept. The power cut last night screwed up the alarm. I was going to work from home today anyway, but you're going to be late." While Lars' words were hard to take in, Ben noticed that Lars looked tired. His normally ruddy skin was pale, and he had bags under his eyes. "I'll get some tea on while you get washed and dressed, then I'll run you to school, okay?" Lars was out of the door before Ben could protest that he didn't want to go to school.

Still muzzy-headed, Ben staggered to his feet.

Automatically, he went to draw the curtain, but his hand stalled. What would he see if he looked down? Would there be crouching figures by the back door? Don't be ridiculous, he thought. It's daylight. Even so, he couldn't help glancing down.

Sunlight bathed the garden. In the harsh light of day, the willow looked butchered, its limbs tangled, its roots exposed, a large crater gouged in the lawn. The sunlight did not seem to penetrate the woods beyond the garden; they looked dark and forbidding.

"Tea's ready!" Lars' voice bulled its way up the stairs, setting off an ache in Ben's head that flared with each movement as he stripped off his dirty clothes, grabbed fresh ones and made for the bathroom. As he passed his dirty jeans, his foot caught them, sending them skidding on the polished wooden floor. There was a clunk as they hit the wall. Ben reached down and felt in the pocket, retrieving the hag stones he had found the day before. He hefted their weight thoughtfully before putting them in the pocket of his clean pants.

Neither Ben nor Lars spoke on the journey to school. Ben wondered if Lars was giving him the silent treatment deliberately, if he had finally pushed him too far. But if that was the case, Lars would have left him to take the consequences of missing school. He glanced sideways at Lars, but his face gave nothing away as he concentrated on guiding the small car around the ring road.

As they drew up in front of the school, Ben looked at the clock on the dashboard. Nearly twelve.

Lars followed his glance to the clock. "Shit. Maybe I should have written you a note. Do you want me to come in and explain?"

"Nah. If they give me any trouble, you can write me one tomorrow." Even as he spoke, a plan was forming in Ben's mind. He'd wait until Lars drove off, then make his way back to the woods. He had to find out what had happened to Wyliff and Billy Blind. It was risky, particularly if Lars was going to be home, but it could be done. It had to be done — preferably in daylight.

Trying to keep his voice casual, Ben asked, "So, uh, what are you going to do today, Lars? Sure you don't need to go to the university?" Shit, he thought, too obvious. When had he ever shown any interest in Lars' comings and goings?

Lars sighed. "I was just going to write up my notes on the churches we visited yesterday, but I'm not really in the mood. I've got to sort out the willow tree, too. I said I'd call a tree surgeon, but I really should get in touch with Professor Parker, let him know what's happened." He looked directly at Ben as if seeking confirmation of some sort. "Maybe I'll head off to Norwich — I'm halfway there already — go hang with the Green Men in the cathedral."

"Why not?" Ben said, and got out of the car. Just before he closed the door, on a sudden impulse, he drew the stones out of his pocket and thrust the tan one toward Lars. "Take this," he said, slamming the door before he could change his mind or Lars could speak.

The night had been running, running, running. Pounding the earth, no stopping. Where was the hob? Where was the boy? Running, running, running.

The willow was down. Its ebbing life force jangled Wyliff's senses, made it hard to think. But there was an oak. Oak is strength. He leaned against it, feeling his pulse calm, his leaves still. Daylight was good. The Fey were not at ease in sunshine; only Jazriel forced himself to bear it. Sun is safety.

The cottage was empty, but Wyliff caught the taint of Jazriel's minion. He had been here, and others like him. How many? A quiver of panic, a rustle of leaves, sap rising. Wyliff's fingers found the bark of the oak, felt for cracks, felt for calm. Where was the boy? Where was the hob? The hob he lost in the first flight, when they ran from the clearing, surprised by Jazriel. The boy had not been there yesterday, had come just as Jazriel worked his weather magick, killing the willow, forcing them to flee.

Where was the boy? He needed the boy. Where was the hob? He needed the hob.

Lars took forever, staring at the stone Ben had given him, holding it up to his face and peering through the hole. Ben crouched behind the hedge, watching him, muttering, "Go, damn it — just go!"

"Talking to yourself, Larsson! Not a good sign, not good at all, particularly when hiding behind a hedge like some kind of sex pervert."

Ben reared up in shock, almost colliding with Rob Fanshawe, who was peering down at him. He staggered back, falling against the hedge, feeling its sharp twigs poke his back.

"Whoa, jumpy!" Rob held his hands up as if to ward off something. "Perhaps with good reason." He smiled at Ben, a rather knowing smirk that Ben didn't like.

"What do you mean?" Ben extricated himself from the hedge and brushed himself down, trying to look nonchalant while calculating how quickly he could get rid of Rob — and school.

Rob surprised him by saying, "Wanna go to the chippy around the corner and get something for lunch? I'll tell you what you missed this morning." Before Ben could reply, he added, "And, you *were* missed this morning. Greengrass came and talked to the whole sixth form. The police, too. They took a roll call, so you'd better make sure you square that away with him after lunch."

Ben shook his head. "I'm not staying. My old man dropped me off, but I was just waiting for him to leave —

then I was going to head home. I don't feel like school today, but I couldn't tell him that," he offered, hoping Rob would just let him go.

"You might want to rethink that."

"Why?"

Rob looked over his shoulder. Ben followed the direction of his gaze. Among the students spilling out of the school as lunch break started, looking directly at them, was Mr. Greengrass.

"Shit! If I don't turn up after lunch, he'll be straight on the phone to Lars."

"Come on, let's go get those chips." Rob started walking and Ben followed, feeling as if Greengrass's eyes were burning his back.

The fish and chip shop was crowded and steamy, the smell of frying making Ben realize how hungry he was — it was almost twenty-four hours since he had eaten. As he and Rob placed their orders, he realized that some of the students were staring at him — not even trying to disguise their curiosity.

"Why is everyone staring at me?" he asked Rob, once they had taken their greasy paper packages of chips out to the grass verge by the side of the road.

"You were one of the missing" was Rob's amused reply.

"What? The 'missing'? What the hell's that all about?"

Rob looked sideways at Ben. "You really don't know, do you?" He shook his head in disbelief. "It was all over the local papers — even made some of the nationals — and the TV. Don't Canadians follow the news?"

Ben shook his head. He tried to remember the last time he or Lars had turned on the television and couldn't — it would mean sitting together in the small front room. Lars usually worked at the kitchen table, and Ben spent as much time as he could in his room.

"Well," Rob said, drawing out the word with relish. "Norwich is just a hot spot of happenings the last few days, and somehow it's all passed you by." He shoved a chip into his mouth, chewed noisily, watching Ben to see if his words would have any effect. When Ben just stared, he went on. "Yeah, Friday night, some kids from our school went out, and they've not come back."

"Who?" Ben cursed himself. His voice was too loud, too eager.

"A group of fifth years," Rob said, "including that strange little wanker Baz who had a go at you last week. Him and a couple of his friends. I think they've just done a bunk myself, but the police have been called in now. They were asking if any of us knew anything or had seen them since Friday." He snorted. "Like we'd have anything to do with those head cases! Or help the police." Crumpling up his chip paper, he tossed it at a nearby rubbish bin. "He shoots! He scores!" Rob said. "Anyway, that's the reason for the roll calls. I figure each year head will be making a list of anyone absent whose folks haven't called, make sure they're not 'missing,' too."

Ben's thoughts whirled. Here was confirmation that the world of the Fey and his own familiar world were beginning to merge — and that terrible things would happen if it wasn't stopped. He got to his feet slowly, feeling a tremor in the core of his being.

Oblivious to Ben's distress, Rob continued talking as they made their way back to the school. "And it's not only people missing — there's all this weird weather shit that happened yesterday. In the *Eastern Daily Press* this morning, it was like they didn't know which to give the front page to, the missing kids or some mini-tornado that touched down in several places. Couldn't have been a big deal, though. Worst that happened was in Cringleford." Rob stopped walking, grabbed Ben's arm. "Hey, that's where you live, isn't it? Did you see it? Was it amazingly cool?"

Ben shook off Rob's hand roughly. He didn't like Rob's almost voyeuristic interest. Would Rob be like Baz, easily seduced by the power of the Fey? Ben shuddered at the thought.

"No need to be like that," Rob said, negotiating his way around the huddle of smokers just off school property. "I'm just interested, that's all."

"Yeah, well, you're acting like it's all some big joke. It's not!" He looked over to the school. Mr. Greengrass was still standing on the steps, like a sentinel watching over the students through the lunch break. "I did see it. It wasn't funny. It uprooted the willow tree in our back garden, and it's a mess. Satisfied?" Ben was trying to avoid shouting, but the words were coming out in an angry hiss.

Rob took a step away from Ben.

"And, yeah, Baz is a little shit, but he has a family, too. Think how they must feel, wondering where he is, what might have happened to him. And what about Yvonne Lea? Is she just another *happening*?"

Rob was definitely backing away now, but he spoke as he went. "Who the hell is Yvonne Lea? What's your problem? I was just telling you what happened. Maybe you've got something to hide. Maybe the police should be talking to you. After all, you were in a fight with Baz and now he's missing! Maybe you're having a go at me, so people don't connect you to all this strange stuff? Maybe that's what you're doing here. But I'm not having any of it, so piss off!" He turned abruptly and walked away.

Oh, I'm connected all right, Ben thought.

"Ben! Ben Larsson!" Mr. Greengrass's voice cut through Ben's thoughts, and he turned to see the teacher waving him over. There was no way out. He had to go over.

"You weren't in school this morning?" The question

was mild in tone, but one look at Greengrass's face told Ben he had to answer.

"Yeah, I'm sorry," he said, trying to sound it. "We got hit by that storm last night, knocked out our power. So the alarm didn't go off. My dad and I slept in. He brought me as soon as he could," he added, hoping that this would head off more questions, "but it was lunchtime so I went with Rob Fanshawe for some chips."

Greengrass's face looked troubled.

"We're allowed to leave the school property at lunch, aren't we?" Ben asked.

"Yes, yes," Mr. Greengrass said impatiently. "Did Fanshawe tell you what's happened? That some of our pupils are missing?"

Ben nodded, hoping Greengrass would leave it at that.

"The police have asked that if anyone has any information they should come forward." Here Greengrass looked shrewdly at Ben. "But you wouldn't even know any of the missing boys, would you?" He left his question hanging. Then, with an abrupt, forced jollity, he asked, "So, how's school going, Ben? Settling in? Looked like you and Fanshawe were having a bit of a disagreement. Nothing serious, I hope." Looking down at his watch, he said, "It's almost time for the bell. Why don't you tell me about it while we walk down to your classroom?"

Where were they? The sun was taking on the gold of late afternoon. He shifted uneasily, each foot making a sucking noise as he lifted it from the soft humus under the oak tree. He had watched the house all day, but it had no life.

He had thought, though, long and hard, the ideas forming like acorns in his head, and now he knew what must be done. But he needed the boy. He needed the hob, too.

With only the movement of his eyes betraying his presence, Wyliff watched the man come into the garden, followed by others, strangers who walked the length of the willow. Their words were lost to him, but the things they carried, things with edges and metal teeth, made him shudder.

The sound of an animal in pain, a roaring scream drilled through his head, but no animal was there. Just the men and the things swarming the willow, teeth ripping into its flesh, dismembering it.

Birds rose from the treetops and took flight. Wyliff watched them, wishing he could leave, too. He watched the birds until they were tiny specks in the sky, like pollen grains, watched them so he did not have to watch the men, and the things, and what once had been the willow.

Ben slammed into the hallway, his bag hitting the wall with a thump. Bloody Greengrass! He had walked Ben right to the very door of his classroom, like he was escorting a prisoner, probing with oh-so-gentle questions about what friends Ben had made, until he had worked his way round to the fight. Greengrass knew that his assailant had been Baz, and now that Baz was missing, he was trying to gather any information that he could. Ben had given nothing away. What was the point? Who would have believed him?

He could hear Lars puttering in the kitchen, whistling tunelessly. Ben longed to head straight out, but Lars' head appeared around the door.

"There's some tea in the pot and some cookies I bought in Norwich. Want some?"

Ben followed Lars into the kitchen, which was surprisingly tidy even though Mrs. Lea had not been back since Yvonne's collapse. He still hadn't got used to how meticulous and neat Lars was with everything — except his own appearance, of course. Today the contrast was more evident than usual. Perhaps because of the rush that morning, Lars hadn't tied back his hair in its usual braid or ponytail. It hung loose, a thick wavy mass that came halfway down his back — its life and vibrant color contrasting with his pale, tired face A pang pierced Ben as it reminded him of Yvonne's pale face awash in her sea of red hair. He shuddered.

"Someone walking over your grave, Ben?" Lars asked.

"Nah," Ben said, liberating a handful of cookies from the plate that Lars had placed in the middle of the table. "Just a bit cold — tired, too." He nearly added "after last night," but he didn't want to get back to the never-ending discussion of how he was, and what Lars could do to make things better between them.

"School okay?" Lars' voice was determinedly neutral. "Didn't give you a hard time about being late?"

"Nope. I saw Mr. Greengrass, explained we'd slept in." Ben took the cup of tea that Lars offered, but he had to force himself not to gulp it down. He couldn't stop himself from looking at the back door, thinking about what might lie beyond it and how long it would be before he could go and find out.

"Cool. Glad everything's copacetic." Lars said nothing more, just munched on his cookie, taking swigs of tea to wash it down. A scattering of crumbs was lodged in his beard and mustache. Ben sighed with relief. Lars still didn't know about the disappearances. Just as well. He wouldn't try to stop him from going out.

He stood up. "Thanks for the tea. I'm going out for a walk. I'll do my homework after dinner."

An expression that Ben couldn't read flitted across Lars' face. "Sure," he said, "but be careful — in case other trees have been weakened by the storm."

Ben grabbed a sweatshirt from the back of his chair and made for the door. It was almost too easy.

"Ben, one question before you go." Lars spoke quietly, almost in a monotone.

Shit. He composed his face into what he hoped was a neutral mask.

Lars was regarding him steadily. "Why did you give me that stone today?" A derisive laugh almost forced its way from Ben's throat, but he turned it into a cough. Was Lars going sentimental on him? Shit!

"A whim," he said coldly, "that's all. Don't flatter yourself that it's anything more than that, okay?"

Lars gave him one of the big, beaming smiles that revealed the gap between his two front teeth and made him look like a goofy nine-year-old. "That's what I thought," he said and reached for another cookie. "Just be back for supper."

A shudder ran through Wyliff's frame and vibrated up the trunk of the oak against which he leaned. Brown leaves drifted down from the tree, adding to the pile that already covered his feet. The boy was walking toward him, the dying sun behind him dressing him in gold. Wyliff raised a hand and then slid around the trunk, away from the eyes of the house. He heard the rapid footfalls that brought the boy closer.

"Wyliff, you're okay!" Ben flung his arms around the Green Man, then wished he hadn't. It was as if Wyliff had been electrocuted, his long limbs thrashed and danced. Ben released his grip and stepped back. "Sorry, sorry. I didn't think. I'm just so happy to see you. Baz, Jazriel's boy, said that he had been sent for me while Jazriel hunted you and Billy Blind. I've been so worried. I wanted to be here earlier, but I couldn't get away."

Wyliff blinked. "The touch of you, the smell of you — all are strange. They tantalize and they disgust." He touched Ben's face, jerking back after the lightest contact. "You are whole, not damaged. This is good, because tonight we must take back that which has been stolen."

Ben sighed. He was becoming used to Wyliff's gnomic utterances, but it was almost impossible to have a linear conversation, in which decisions were made.

Wyliff slid down the oak until he was sitting. "We talk, then we go." Wyliff looked up at Ben until he sat cross-legged facing him. Wyliff then looked down at him from his lankiness but said nothing.

Okay, Ben thought, he wants me to talk first. So that was what Ben did, pouring out all that had happened the day before — the uprooting of the willow, the encounter with Baz and the conclusions he had drawn. Throughout Ben's recitation, Wyliff said nothing, but he smiled once. The leaves around Wyliff's mouth fluttered first, almost as if they were being blown back to reveal his mouth. His lips, full and brown, parted to reveal sturdy teeth, green as grass. When Ben finally stopped talking, Wyliff still did not speak.

"So, am I right?" Ben demanded in exasperation. "Jazriel's taking his power from humans like Baz, when he should be taking it from the natural world. And what about Yvonne? Is she like some super reservoir of power that he wants, but needs her to co-operate? For fuck's sake, say something! Help me understand. Tell me what we can do." Ben's voice had risen to an anguished wail that Wyliff responded to rather than the words. He covered his ears with his hands.

"Seelie has become unseelie, and unseelie drains without thought for what must remain. The girl has been marked, has been groomed since she was a twig. She would be Queen Oak to Jazriel's King Oak. He holds her bound until she agrees. Then he will take her." Wyliff's eyes welled with amber tears. "Fear what such a union would unleash upon the world, boy. Their child — unseelie with the savagery of the human. Fey will become human, and human will become Fey. Unseelie all!"

Ben felt sick, remembering the mute appeal that had been in Yvonne's eyes when she had tried to talk to him at school, the strain on her face as she sat imprisoned upon the crystal throne. He was revolted as he remembered Billy Blind saying that Jazriel and his cohorts had made a pet of Yvonne when she was a child and wondered whether the hob was hinting at something far worse, which would explain Yvonne's fragility and alienation from the human world. He jumped to his feet, started pacing, kicking at the fallen leaves.

"He controlled me like the dog he called me, you're scared shitless of fire, the hob is small and weak. What the fuck can we do?" Even as he spoke, Ben knew the Green Man had already thought it out — the disconcerting smile was back as he levered himself upright, his long, strangely jointed legs unfolding like ladders.

"Like against like was my plan," Wyliff said simply. "Jazriel uses his human. I would use you, take your power."

A wash of fear swept through Ben. He pictured Baz as he had last seen him, a diminished presence, twitching. Would he end up like that? He had thought that Wyliff was the good guy in this whole mess, but what had led him to believe that Wyliff cared about him? The Green Man was obsessed with preserving the status quo. Who says he'd care any more than Jazriel did about the means he used?

"Like against unlike is better," Wyliff continued. "It is better to give freely than to take by trickery. Jazriel has my measure. You, he does not know. I will give you my power and you will confront him." He smiled broadly. "It may not come to this. Tonight the Unseelie Court will feast. It will be a good time to take the girl back, while little attention is paid." Wyliff started to walk deeper into the woods.

"Just hold on!" Ben shouted. "I haven't agreed to anything. I don't know how to use your power."

"If we get the girl, we will have time to learn and to practice. Now is not for talking, but for doing. We must go." Wyliff grabbed Ben's hand, shivering slightly at its touch.

Ben had the stretching sensation and found himself on the other side of the woods, looking out on a flat, sloping field that led down to a stream. He and Lars had walked here one evening soon after they came. There was a faint rumble that puzzled Ben until he realized it was the traffic leaving Norwich on the Cringleford Bypass. It was twilight, the sky was darkening and becoming opaque. So much for being back for supper. Ben hoped Lars would just assume that he was in a sulk and not come looking for him.

Wyliff was watching the center of the field, where the darkness seemed to be thickening. As Ben strained to make it out, details became clearer. Fantastically draped tents, or pavilions, were appearing like a sudden excrescence of mushrooms. They should have been beautiful, with their silk banners and fanciful shapes, but there was something distorted about them that jarred the eye. It was not only the shapes, but the colors, too: reds that had the blackish hue of dried blood; the yellows of bile and pus; livid and lurid greens, like the bacteria that grows on rotted food.

Weaving through the mismatched colors of the pavilions, Ben could now make out the tall figures of the Fey, in black or dark gray.

"Seelie becomes unseelie," he muttered. He glanced sideways, but the Green Man was intent on what was unfolding in front of them and paid him no mind.

In the central space among the pavilions, Ben could now see tables appearing, laden with strange-colored fruits dripping from plates made of what looked like black marble, and wooden bowls of hazelnuts and berries.

A sudden movement near Wyliff's head caught Ben's attention. The wren he had once seen hiding in the leaves that wreathed Wyliff's head had landed on Wyliff's shoulder. It nestled there against the Green Man's bark, its tiny chest heaving. Then it flew up to his head, making a thin piping sound. Wyliff whistled something back. The bird looked down at Ben, its eyes like tiny black currants, before disappearing into Wyliff's foliage.

"The girl is in the far one." Wyliff pointed to a pavilion that stood somewhat apart from the others and was shaped like a small castle with a turret and crenellations fashioned out of cloth. It was the icy blue of lips and limbs exposed too long to the cold.

"How do you know that?" Ben asked, and laughed. "A little bird told you, right?"

The Green Man's face was rigid when he turned it to Ben. "Why is this amusing to you? It also told me that the human boys were left guarding her, but one trails around after Jazriel and the other two are asleep, spent of their power." Wyliff sighed. "I had hoped the hob would be here. Have you seen the hob? He is good at making a nuisance of himself. A nuisance would have been a good diversion."

Ben shook his head, trying to hold down the flare of worry as he remembered Baz's glee at Jazriel hunting Wyliff and the "little feller." Then anger joined the worry — was that all the Green Man had to say about the hob? Didn't he care what had happened to him? That he was being hunted because of Wyliff's actions?

"No matter." Wyliff's words were chilling in their indifference. Wyliff pointed to Ben and then to himself. "We will travel under a glamour. It will fool the humans, and we will hope that we do not encounter the Fey."

Ben had no idea what Wyliff meant, but saw, flowing upward from his feet, an image of a young Fey man. Wyliff himself appeared to be shrinking into a stately older Fey whose garments were only faintly tinged with gray. Awe replaced anger, and Ben became lost in the intricacies of the trick. If he concentrated hard, he could make out, like faint shadows, their own forms deep within the Fey images. Ben reached into his pocket, fingering the hag stone.

"This is not the time for staring." There was a touch of asperity in Wyliff's tone as he brought them right outside the blue pavilion.

Ben peered cautiously around — the Fey all seemed to be clustered around someone or something on the far side of the feasting space. Ben looked around to see if Wyliff had noticed, but he was fumbling with the ties that closed the pavilion doors, struggling to pull apart the complex knots that seemed almost to writhe in protest.

With a sharp exhalation of breath, Wyliff finally succeeded. Warily, he parted the flaps of the pavilion, motioning Ben to follow him.

Their caution was unnecessary. Both of Baz's friends lay in some sort of stupor, just inside. The slackness of their limbs, their careless, even uncomfortable positions seemed to indicate that they had fallen suddenly. Ben gingerly put his fingers to the side of one boy's neck. There was a pulse, but it was very faint. He could see how worn the boy looked, his skin dry, with tiny lines around the eyes and mouth. His face was deathly pale.

"Leave him!" Wyliff's words were whip-sharp. "He is of no importance. We are here for her."

As Ben stood up, his eyes widened in shock. Around the flimsy walls of the pavilion were bodies, stacked like firewood. All were older Fey, as far as Ben could tell, swathed in the same cobweb bindings that Ben had seen around the old man, Jazriel's father. He scanned their faces, trying to find that old man, but his memory of him was too vague, too fragmented. All had the same eyes, eyes that burned with impotent fury as they followed him to the shadowy back of the pavilion where Wyliff was standing. Against the back wall, in a space free of bodies, was the crystal throne, now the dark purple-black of a bruise. Yvonne's face was still rigid, but in her open eyes Ben saw recognition, then a pleading look. She still wore the thorn-decked dress, but now the beads of blood had become trickles, staining the gray cobwebby material.

Ben rushed forward to pull her free of the chair. She made no reply, but looked down at her wrists. She was bound to the chair at her wrists and ankles by thorn-encrusted briars that grew from the chair itself. She had obviously struggled, as her wrists and ankles were bloody and rubbed raw. Steeling himself against the pain, Ben grasped the briars binding Yvonne's wrists and pulled, wincing as the thorns cut into his palms. They did not move.

"This is good," Wyliff said as he peered over Ben's shoulder. "Thorn, however it has been corrupted, is good. Thorn I command. Metal or leather would have been bad." Ben saw the glamour around Wyliff waver, almost pulse. Gradually, very gradually, the briar strands uncoiled themselves. The decorative thorns on Yvonne's dress clattered like tiny teeth as they fell onto the chair. As she collapsed forward, Ben only just managed to catch her.

"She is not with us now." Wyliff regarded him gravely as Ben tried to lift Yvonne. "Her spirit hides. I will carry her as we leave. Leave is what we must do now."

Ben wasn't inclined to argue, even though it made his heart ache to leave the others imprisoned. For this, he realized, was what the pavilion was — a prison to hold those who opposed Jazriel's way. He started to speak — if they stayed just a few minutes longer to free the others, perhaps they might help them oppose Jazriel — but the Green Man was shifting his feet as if anxious to go. Desperately trying to order his thoughts, Ben concentrated on what he wanted most — to be as far away as possible from this place. If they got Yvonne away safely, that was all that mattered. He would have done what was needed. Everything from then on would be Wyliff's problem alone. Ben winced at how easily he had been controlled. Confronting the Fey prince terrified him, and now, well, maybe it wouldn't be necessary. He held Yvonne steady as Wyliff gently scooped her into his arms.

Outside the pavilion, there was a sudden noise, the sound of running feet, shouts and the baying of hounds. Wyliff looked at Ben, raised one long finger to his lips. In a hoarse whisper he said, "We will move out quietly, then run — back to the safety of the trees."

Ben nodded. The noise outside was getting louder, as if there was a chase weaving among the pavilions.

Cautiously, Ben and Wyliff edged out of the pavilion, only to see a pack of Fey heading straight for them. A shriek of alarm escaped before Ben could clamp his mouth shut, but he quickly realized that the Fey were not interested in them. Just ahead of the pack, with the black hound and the white, red-eared one nipping at his heels, a small figure galloped, screaming curses as he ran.

Billy Blind!

He saw them and dodged around them. As he sped past, Ben saw his face was covered with cuts and what looked like burns. Ben tried to call out, but the words were trapped in his throat as the Fey ran into them, causing them to go down in a tumble of limbs. He reached out a desperate hand, trying to keep contact with either Yvonne or Wyliff, but there were too many bodies, all trying to right themselves. When he finally made it to his feet, there was no sign of Wyliff. Yvonne lay on the ground, Baz and a group of Fey looking down at her.

Ben made a lunge for her, but Jazriel interposed himself, looking down at him, a mocking smile splitting his thin face.

"Nice try, human, but your cowardly friends seem to have abandoned you." His laugh slid up the scale to a high-pitched giggle that hurt Ben's ears. "So, what is the result of your heroics? I still have my queen." The words slid off his tongue, Jazriel savoring their sound. "Her will is weakening, and now," his smile broadened as he said in a tone of false surprise, "I have you, too! How fortuitous. I'm sure I can find a Fey woman who would enjoy a human plaything, especially one with the old blood, the blood of heroes." A click of his fingers froze Ben in place, just as he tried to bolt for the trees. "Don't be foolish. I've learned. I know what your power is and how to contain it, especially with the help of my little friend here." Jazriel reached behind him and pulled Baz to his side — a horrible, shambling parody of himself.

"Put them back." A lordly wave of a languid hand brought a group of Fey scurrying. Ben found himself roughly carried into the pavilion. He was tossed like a lump of wood on some cushions that lay to one side of the crystal throne, landing so that he was able to watch as Yvonne was carefully placed back in it, Jazriel fussing over the folds of her dress as if she were some beautiful doll. Jazriel made a gesture, and thin filaments of what looked like silver oozed from the throne, braiding themselves into manacles that tightly bound her wrists and ankles. Needlelike silver points appeared on her dress in place of the thorns.

"Well, that's that, isn't it?" Jazriel said, looking around at the assembled Fey. "We have what we wanted. The hob may have got away, but he is small meat anyway.

The tree man is terrified of us. Could life get any better?" He spread his arms wide as he looked around at his followers. Seeing Ben struggling against his invisible bonds, Jazriel said, "There's no point, human boy. I am too strong now."

Jazriel's words slammed into Ben.

Then the whole world went green.

Something was tickling his ear. Ben shook his head, trying to dislodge whatever it was, but the tickling started up again. No, not a tickling, a jabbing, as if someone was tapping the fleshy lobe of his ear with a blunt needle.

He gingerly opened his eyes, closed them immediately in horror. He opened them again very slowly. Nothing looked right. It was like peering through one of those old green wine bottles. He wasn't even sure that there were words to describe the colors he now saw. He was still lying on the floor, but Yvonne's throne prison was no longer there. Baz's two cronies were also gone. He and the imprisoned Fey were all that remained in the pavilion, but his view of them had changed, too. Ben still saw their bodies, but he also saw that a nimbus of light flared around each one. No two were the same color, but each nimbus matched a small flamelike core that burned where he supposed the heart would be. Burned. Was that the right word? He didn't know, but each core was lined in an ashy gray that contained the fire, deadening it, muting it.

What the hell was happening? Had he banged his head somehow? Were these strange visual effects the result of a concussion, or some sort of brain injury?

Ben tried moving his head, shaking it gently to restore the world to normal. Nothing changed. The jabbing sensation near his ear became difficult to ignore. As he lifted his head, something fluttered and came to rest on the cushion directly in front of his face. It was Wyliff's wren little head cocked to one side as it stared into Ben's eyes. Its beak opened and closed and from its throat came the same piping that Ben had heard when it had communicated with Wyliff, only this time, Ben heard words in the piping. He shuddered, feeling sick and shaky. When the wave of nausea passed, Ben forced himself to listen closely to what the creature was saying.

"It is time, boy. Time to confront. Time to restore." These were Wyliff's words — the wren was nothing but a conduit. Relief surged through Ben, a powerful tide that made tears come to his eyes. Wyliff had not abandoned him.

The relief sung in Ben's voice. "Wyliff, where are you? What's wrong with me? Jazriel zapped me again." He started to laugh then at the absurdity of having only the language of video games to describe something so terrible.

The wren hopped backward. "You have the power. Look inward."

Ben felt like howling in frustration. He just didn't understand.

Then he saw it — a green flame burning fiercely in his chest. Surrounding his body was an emerald light shot through with gold, pulsing and crackling with power. He worked his mind around it, feeling for it, trying to connect. Images flooded his brain: trees arched and branched through a green world without buildings where a balance was maintained; humans were mere irritants on its periphery. He saw Wyliff and others like him imbued with the same green life force that now suffused his body.

"You did it!" Ben said. "You've given me your power!" Focusing his heart flame, he tried battering Jazriel's binding. He met resistance, tried again, allowing no other thoughts to intrude upon his mind. Like rotted cloth, he felt it give way. Freed, Ben stood up, not quite in control of his body.

The wren launched itself to Ben's shoulder, where it trilled insistently in his ear. "Mine, but no longer mine." Ben detected a hint of sadness in Wyliff's words. "See, the color has changed."

"Where's Yvonne?"

"The time has come when Jazriel feels she will bend to his will. He wants his triumph to be witnessed by all. Go and I will guide you."

Ben moved to the entry of the pavilion, feeling

Wyliff's energy surge through him with each step, strengthening him. There, he hesitated, ignoring Wyliff's protest that there was no time for delay. He turned back, searching the faces of the Fey there. One was a little apart. Was that Jazriel's father? Havriel, that was the name that Billy Blind had called him. Ben walked over, a plan forming in his mind. He placed his hand upon the Fey's chest, directly above the flame at his heart, a flame the deep, glowing red of an ember. He willed the power to flow through his hand, hoping that it would break through the bindings that Jazriel had placed. Ben was jolted backward, almost as if Wyliff's power had hit a solid wall. Havriel's flamelike core flared briefly against the gray ring surrounding it, but then died down.

"Stupid idea," Ben muttered. So much for his vision of arriving to face Jazriel at the head of a group of enraged Fey. He turned away in disgust, ignoring the wren flying in circles around him, piping and cheeping. He didn't see it hover in front of Havriel, whose heart flame had begun to glow more strongly.

It was true night now, Ben realized, as he emerged from the pavilion. How long had he lain there? What time had passed in the normal world? And what would Lars be thinking?

A shout of high-pitched laughter rang out, and Ben turned his attention to the feasting area. Lights blazed around the Fey. There was no sign of Baz, but his two friends lay to one side, their faces ashen, as if all life had been sucked from them. The wren warbled in Ben's ear, its tiny, shrill voice at odds with the heaviness of Wyliff's words, which it delivered. "Triumph makes for carelessness. He is not expecting anything. This is our strength."

"Yeah, right. Fine for you to say," Ben whispered, "but what exactly am I supposed to do? March up to Jazriel and say 'Give me Yvonne, or else!'?"

"Look inward" was all Wyliff said.

Ben drew in a deep breath. His mouth was suddenly very dry. Stumbling a little on the rough, tussocky grass, he forced himself forward until he reached the Fey. They were intently looking at something in the center of the feasting area and, at first, paid him no attention. But as he drew close, some turned as if sensing his presence. One hissed and drew back. Like the ripples on a pond from a thrown stone, awareness moved through the throng.

Jazriel, at the center, was the last to see him. He was bent over Yvonne, who lolled in the crystal throne. Ben was horrified to see the slackness of her features. Her eyes were half open and tears ran from them. Jazriel was removing the silver manacles from her wrists. Baz, who was loitering at Jazriel's side, alerted him by pulling on one of his trailing black sleeves. Jazriel jerked his arm away, swatting at Baz's hand as one would an insect, but Baz persisted until Jazriel looked up. Surprise twisting his features, it was only seconds before he raised his hands to paralyze Ben, again.

"Look inward." The wren relayed Wyliff's words endlessly, a looping chant that blocked out everything else.

Ben found the still center of himself, the green flame, seized it with his mind and pushed it outward. He saw the halo of green around his body flare and harden, battering back the surge of Jazriel's power, a lance of purple light aimed at his heart.

Jazriel dropped his hands instantly and stared at Ben. "I have to give you credit, Tree Man," he said. "This is inventive. Make the human the puppet, and absent yourself from harm or danger."

"I am no one's puppet!"

The look of shock on Jazriel's face when he heard Ben's hoarse and ragged voice told Ben it was Wyliff's voice that he had expected to hear.

Without knowing quite what he was doing or how he did it, Ben caught up Jazriel's power, roughly shaped it and threw it back in Jazriel's face.

The Fey staggered a little, almost tripping over Baz. He steadied himself with a hand on Baz's shoulder. Baz stiffened, his body jerking in little spasms as Jazriel drew power from him. With his free hand, Jazriel pointed at Ben.

"Inward, inward, inward." Ben wasn't sure whether he was hearing his own thoughts or Wyliff's words. As purple fire raced toward him once more, he braced himself, concentrating on creating a defensive shield to protect himself before he tried another attack.

It was as if someone had punched him in the stomach. Ben felt himself catapulted backward, arms and legs flailing, his fall stopped only by a wall of the Fey. Hands reached out, grasping and tearing at him, as he tried to free himself and regain his balance.

"Leave him. The tree man has sent him to challenge me alone." Jazriel's voice rang out, dripping with authority, but the effect was spoiled when he gave the high-pitched giggle that had so unnerved Ben earlier. "After all, am I not honorable in all my dealings?"

The hands dropped away. Ben found himself once more facing Jazriel, whose glittering violet eyes were fixed avidly on him. The wren returned to his shoulder but remained silent.

Drawing in a deep breath, Ben looked around. Yvonne's eyes were fully open, looking directly at him. "I don't know if this will work," he muttered. Then the time for words was gone.

With his fingers gouging into Baz's shoulder, Jazriel sent a wall of purple roiling toward Ben. He met it with Wyliff's green, the two magicks clashing like boulders, neither giving way. Ben felt himself grow very still. He closed his eyes, not wanting anything to take his mind from holding steady. He felt the soft feathers of the wren on his neck. The little bird's breathing was in time with the pulses of power he sent out from deep inside himself to match Jazriel's. Every muscle was strained and rigid. He could sense each time Jazriel took power from Baz, feel the increased pressure, the weakening. He was not sure how long he could keep this up, but knew that he must, until Baz had no more to give. He only prayed that Wyliff would last that long, too. "Wyliff," he whispered, without hope of an answer.

"Ben! Ben! Where the hell are you?"

The familiar voice snapped Ben's eyes open. He struggled to stay upright as Jazriel battered him, sending burning purple flames through his bones and nerves, yet leaving no mark. He sensed rather than heard Wyliff's keening anguish entwined with his own. His mind seemed detached, taking in inconsequential details, as if taking him away from the agony.

Lars. Lars burst through the troop of Fey, head down, arms swinging, bellowing Ben's name. His face was crimson, as if he had been running. Ben found himself idly wondering how Lars could see the Fey, and then he remembered the hag stone that he had given him earlier. Lars must have shoved it into a pocket. His father was trying to reach him, battling through the Fey, who laughed, tripped him, even turned him around so that he lost his way. Held in place by pain, Ben watched helplessly.

Lars' long hair streamed behind him, like some Viking warrior of legend, Ben thought, and he even seemed to be making some headway, lashing out at those tormenting him. Ben wanted to shout "Forget it! Go! Save yourself!" but the words remained locked in his throat.

Jazriel allowed Lars to get close to Ben. Then he struck, skeins of purple flames winding around Lars and rooting him to the spot, leaving only his face capable of movement, showing an almost incandescent fury as he struggled to free himself.

"How touching!" Leaning on Baz, Jazriel moved closer. "The bear comes looking for his cub." He put his face close to Lars', twisting his elegant features into a mocking parody of Lars' teeth-baring grimace. "Very fierce. I tremble. See how I tremble?" Jazriel pretended to cuff Lars playfully, but the white imprint of the Fey's hand appeared on Lars' scarlet cheek as if he had been stung. Tentatively, Ben reached out with his mind, trying to find Wyliff. The wren shuddered violently as it raised itself up to take flight. The faintest whisper escaped its beak. "One, two become one."

Jazriel was circling Lars like a farmer examining a prize bull. "See the strength here," he said, "the old blood. How much more powerful he is than this mongrel!"

Jazriel flicked a contemptuous finger at Baz, who leaned into it as if it were a caress. Still holding on to Baz, Jazriel reached with his free hand toward Lars' shoulder, his fingers curved in a pincerlike grip.

"Nooooo!" The cry ripped from Ben's throat, spiraled into the air, causing the wren to fly in panicky circles around his head. Ben's mind reached inside himself, seizing the green flame that flickered uncertainly, pulling it free. Underneath was a blazing flame of gold. Ben took it, too, entwined it with the green and threw its full force at Jazriel.

The night exploded with light — no longer Wyliff's strong emerald, but the tender green of the first spring leaves — causing the Fey to draw back in fear.

Ben felt Baz's anguish as Jazriel tried to draw power from him — Baz had no more left to give. Lars shook his head, suddenly freed, and knocked Baz to the ground. Without this support, Jazriel seemed to cave in on himself, shimmering within his envelope of light. A wail went up from the watching Fey, rising in pitch until Ben could no longer hear it, just feel it vibrate through his very being.

A last massive flare illuminated the night, shooting like a comet straight at Jazriel. The Fey prince was lit up from within, his face frozen, openmouthed in terror. Then Ben saw the light recoil, come straight back at him. He could do no more than close his eyes and brace for the impact. He felt the light tear through him. He staggered but did not fall.

When his eyes opened, colors were normal. Looking down, he saw the solid color of his sweatshirt, no glowing light.

Jazriel was gone. Where he had stood was a circle of earth burned free of its grass. In its center stood a sapling.

"It is done. Two became one," the wren fluted near his ear. Then, beating its wings mightily, it made for the woods.

Ben's knees buckled. Before he could fall to the ground, strong arms grabbed him, held him upright. He let himself be drawn into a rough embrace. The coarse wool of Lars' shirt pressed against his face. Lars patted his back in an unfamiliar gesture, his hand landing a bit too heavily for comfort. That well-meaning awkwardness was more than Ben could bear. Tears and sobs were wrenched from him, and he made no effort to check them.

"Bloody hell, it's all done and dusted, isn't it?" The voice was irritated. "You could have waited, especially when I've been racing my arse off all night, trying to round you up some help."

His vision blurred with tears, Ben looked up. Next to Lars was Billy Blind at the head of a small group of hobs who carried sticks, stones and what looked suspiciously like a garden trowel. Out of his battered features, the hob regarded Ben with a steady gaze. How long had Billy Blind been at Jazriel's mercy? Jazriel! The Fey! Ben pulled himself free of Lars, which was not hard, as Lars was staring at the hob, mouth hanging open in shock, as if what he had seen, what he was now seeing, had finally registered.

The Fey were in retreat, but there was an order to it. Colors were flickering around them, shading from dark to light. Standing, stooped in their midst, like a boulder in a stream was Havriel. Looking at Ben with hard, unblinking eyes, Havriel pointed at Lars, then back to Ben. He smiled, but it was a smile that fought with anguish. Ben had to look away; he gazed instead at the sapling, fighting to master his emotions.

When he finally gained control, he looked around the field. As the Fey left, all signs of their presence vanished, too: no pavilions, no Baz. No Yvonne.

"What?" Ben's brain and mouth were not in step. He could not form the questions that seethed inside him. He waited for Lars to start yelling, demanding explanations — maybe then he would get the answers he needed. But Lars was like a statue, only his eyes moving as he stared at the hob. Ben looked questioningly at Billy Blind.

"We hobs have small magick." He smiled. "It'll hold him until the tree man gets here — he has the big magick to put this all to rights." Billy Blind shook his head. "I didn't think you would, but you did it. You and ol' Leaf-face pulled it off." The hob made a mocking bow. "All hail to the hero."

"Yvonne?" Finally, the name forced itself out.

"Ah, the girl! With Jazriel gone, I think she'll be waking up in that hostibal thing right about now."

Now his voice was freed, the questions launched themselves, but Billy Blind dismissed them with an impatient wave of his hand. "Ask the tree man," he said. "He's the one who started this. He can end it. Me and the boys are going to bugger off home and have a few beers. Ah, don't look like that," Billy Blind added. "You did well. Leaf-face might not tell you, so I will." He pointed a stubby finger at Lars. "He did, too — racing through the trees looking for you, not a thought for himself. He's bound to you, and you to him. But you know that. Only you try hard to forget it. Don't do that anymore, bor!" was his final remark as he and the other hobs stomped off toward the woods.

Wyliff ghosted out of the trees a few minutes later, looking as if he had been buffeted by wind. His mane of leaves and vines hung wildly over his face. More leaves had turned from green to the golds and browns of autumn. The wren was perched on his head, where it sat comfortably preening.

"Seelie is seelie again," Wyliff's voice creaked. He kept his eyes on the woods, as if longing for refuge amongst the trees. "Two became one and balance is restored."

Ben sighed. There would be no answers. He looked at Lars, and the Green Man followed his gaze. Wyliff lowered himself ponderously to his knees directly in front of Lars, staring into his eyes, which widened as Lars realized what was in front of him.

Ben almost laughed — he could sense the wonder that Lars felt.

Wyliff raised his hand and with two fingers gently closed Lars' eyes. "Woods are dangerous. It is easy to become lost," he said. Ben saw Lars' lips moving, knew that he was mouthing those words. Then, rising, Wyliff looked over at the tiny sapling.

"Willow," he whispered.

Epilogue

May

Sun glittered on the water of the fjord as Ben tramped along, feeling the sweat trickling through his hair. Ahead of him, Lars and his father were deep in conversation, competing bass baritones that got louder as they started to argue. Whatever it was, it didn't matter — they argued constantly, never with malice, just naturally butting heads. It usually ended when Ben's afi threw up his hands, laughing and saying "Enough!"

Ben liked the laughter. Since they had arrived in Iceland, there had been a lot of laughter. Even he had let loose the odd chuckle. It was hard not to, with Lars even goofier than usual, as if being around his father turned him into an overgrown child. Afi always seemed to wear a slight smile, as if everything was a source of amusement.

England had been different. The months after his confrontation with Jazriel had contained no laughter. Ben tried to work out what was so bleak about them, why they made his insides knot, but there was nothing he could pin down — that time felt as if it had happened to someone else. It had pieces missing and had been twisted to make a version of reality shaped by Wyliff.

Ben had lost track of how many times he heard Lars parrot the words Wyliff had planted in his mind. "Woods are dangerous. It is easy to become lost." He had said them to the doctor he had insisted Ben see the next day. When the doctor had looked puzzled, as if wondering how a teenage boy could get lost in what was, after all, a very small wood, and become so cut and bruised, Lars had repeated them, louder. He had said them to Mr. Greengrass when Ben had returned to school after nearly a week. But that was all he said. Ben was not sure what Wyliff had done to Lars — had he wiped his memories of that night, or just altered them so that they were safe? Ben watched Lars closely, waiting for questions, but they never came, although often he had caught Lars staring out the kitchen window, his eyes fixed on the woods as if looking for something. Lars still carried the hag stone that Ben had given him in his pocket, and it seemed to have become a giant worry bead. When he was lost in introspection, Lars rubbed and fiddled with it.

Ben had found going back to school difficult. Even in the bright Icelandic sunshine, he shivered as he thought of that first day back. Lars had insisted on driving him there, and Ben had not wanted to leave the haven of the little green car. They had sat outside the gate, neither knowing what to say. Finally, he had forced himself to go.

The usual throng had been clustered around the gate, but no one had paid him any attention — it was smooth sailing. And then he had seen Baz, standing by himself, shoulders hunched, eyes fixed on Ben. With an overwhelming urge to flee, Ben had turned around, only to see a flash of green as Lars' car turned the corner. So much for that idea. He had walked on into the school grounds, unable to avoid Baz, who had watched Ben's approach, his face pale, his eyes cold. He looked older. He had raised one hand, but said nothing before turning and walking away, still with the peculiar, hitching limp.

In the common room, Ben had looked for Yvonne. She was out of hospital — her grandmother had called to say so — her illness still a puzzle for the doctors. Mrs. Lea would return to cleaning their house the next week. But Yvonne was not at school. His disappointment, so keen that it made him ache, had surprised him. What had he expected? That she would just show up, restored to health and sanity? That she would rush over to him and shower him with thanks? Sure, right!

His snort of laughter made Lars turn and look at him. He waved a hand to indicate that he was fine. How much credit could he take for freeing Yvonne? Without Wyliff's power, and without Lars knocking Baz away from Jazriel, could he have done it? He would never know, but Yvonne was free. That mattered — even though he had a gut feeling that Yvonne would never fit easily anywhere, not even in her own skin.

To Ben's surprise that first day back at school, people had been talking about Yvonne. Rob Fanshawe, their last antagonistic words forgotten, had called Ben over. "Have you heard the news about your weird girlfriend?"

Ben had been too tired to protest that she was not his girlfriend.

"She came out of her fit or whatever it was, but she's weirder than ever. Phil lives near her, and he said that she won't set foot outside the house, and that when she came home from the hospital, she screamed that she had to get inside, to get away from them. Bizarre!" Rob shook his head, amused.

Ben had felt sick to his stomach but had let the mundane conversation wash over him.

He sighed, quickening his pace to catch up with Lars and Afi. Afi had caught some fish that morning and they were planning to barbecue them for dinner.

Mundane, that was how everything had felt in England — except for the feeling that he *had* achieved something by freeing Yvonne, even though she was now imprisoning herself in the house. He didn't even know what he had been expecting. That Wyliff would be his new best buddy, forever grateful for his help? That he'd have cozy chats with Billy Blind? That a whole new world would be open to him, and only him? But there had been none of that. He had loitered in the woods, hung around in the garden until it became too cold to do so without concocting really weird explanations. Nothing — although there were a few times when the hairs at the base of his neck had stirred, as if he sensed something or he was being watched.

With Lars preoccupied, they had no longer argued. Ben mechanically had done homework, watched TV and, when Lars was not around, worked his way through his father's folklore texts. The same flat mood obviously infected Lars, too — he had carried on with his research in a desultory way, but his enthusiasm had gone. When the letter from Lars' father had arrived in March, asking them to visit him in Iceland, he had come back to life.

"To heck with school. Who cares?" he had said. "You're putting in time anyway. Let's go somewhere new. It's time you met your afi." He had paused, then added, "I think you need to meet him."

And Lars had been right. At first, his afi was just comfortable to be around, an older, less prickly clone of Lars. But one day, when Lars was off visiting a museum, Ben had found himself talking — out of the blue. His afi hadn't asked anything that set him off, but the words came anyway. It seemed as if he had talked all day, and

Afi had listened, nodding occasionally, making a few comments, but understanding. Understanding. "This happens to us, Ben," he had said. "You and I are open to it. Lars, for all his interest, is not yet prepared to deal with it. You must decide whether it is a blessing or a curse." Ben smiled wryly. Probably both.

"Hey, Ben!" Already at the cabin, Lars had emptied the mailbox and now held something in his hand, white, bordered in red and blue — an airmail envelope. "There's a letter for you, from England."

A chill came over Ben. Lars was obviously excited about the letter, probably thought that despite all that had happened, Ben had actually made a friend there, but a curious reluctance slowed Ben down. When he finally took the letter, Lars hovered until Afi pulled on his arm, made him go inside.

Ben took the letter over to the stone that overlooked the fjord's edge. His grandfather sat there to watch the sunset each evening. He turned the letter over in his fingers. It had no return address, but the postmark was Norwich. Ben went to rip the flap open, but there was no need. It had already been opened.

Inside was a folded sheet of notepaper with a short handwritten message, inside that a ragged clipping from a newspaper. Exercising restraint, Ben forced himself to read the note first.

Ben
Don't know why I'm writing to you. I mean, it's not like you even gave me a forwarding address – had to get that from Greengrass. Got nothing to say, really, but I thought you might be interested in this. You always did seem to have a bit of a thing about her.
Rob

There was a brutality about the words that made Ben's heart beat faster as he read the clipping. It was from the *Eastern Daily Press*, dated about two weeks earlier.

MISSING GIRL FOUND

Police made a grisly discovery today in Cringleford. The body of Yvonne Lea, aged seventeen, was found hanging from an oak tree. She had been reported missing two days before by her grandmother, with whom she lived. Miss Lea had been receiving treatment for depression. A police spokesman said that foul play is not suspected.

Ben let the clipping fall from his fingers. He felt hollowed out. Oak. As he crumpled up the envelope,

Acknowledgments

Where does a book begin?

This one, fittingly, has long roots stretching back to my childhood when a love of myth and folktales began. I would like to thank my parents who encouraged me in this, taking me every week to the library, and who were the greatest reading role models, as both read for pleasure in the most matter-of-fact way, a habit that was passed on to all their children.

Some of the books that Lars owns and Ben filches do exist and they were invaluable in creating the non-human characters. K.M. Briggs' *Encyclopaedia of Faries* is a fascinating book. The wonderful English folksinger Mike Harding is a devotee of Green Men, and his Web site is an amazing resource, as is his book of photographs *A Little Book of the Green Man*. He was very generous in sharing his knowledge and pointing me to particular carvings. I hope he approves of Wyliff.

In England, I'd like to thank our friends in Norfolk and Suffolk who were sometimes unwittingly an inspiration. Smith's cottage exists, under a different name, and I have played fast and loose with its garden. My old friend David Pugh took Theo and me to Bungay church and told us the story of the black devil dog. He was also very kind in finding information on other wildmen of East Anglia. Christina Morris was a great source of information about what school would have been like for Ben, speaking as she did from firsthand experience.

In Canada, there are many people to thank.

I was lucky enough to receive financial support from both the Ontario Arts' Council and the Canada Council for the Arts, which gave me time to research and rewrite, just when I needed it.

My thanks as always go to Anne Gray for being my first and most patient reader, my sounding board and a great friend. She is also the one who named Wyliff.

Each of my books with Kids Can Press has been edited by Charis Wahl, and I cannot thank her enough for her keen eye, for keeping me on the straight and narrow and for her friendship.

Finally, I need to thank the Chan boys, Henry and Theo, my own set of father and son. They put up with my obsessions as I write, and sometimes with the domestic chaos that ensues. Without their love and support, I would not be able to do what I do!

something fell from it — a small feather, tangled with strands of long, red hair landed briefly on his knee before being carried away by the wind.

Buds were almost bursting into leaf. Soon, he would no longer need to hide so carefully. Wyliff cast his net of senses wide. All threats had been thwarted, all means removed. All was as it should be.